"You must be hungry.…" **Mary teased with a smile.**

"Starving." Nicholas saw Mary's warm smile and the understanding in her eyes. There was so much he wanted to know about her. His hunger for her was insatiable, he discovered.

"This whole thing…it's like I'm in a living, unfolding dream."

"I understand," Nicholas said. "You feel neither here nor there. You merely float between realms."

Giving him an intense look, Mary said, "Exactly. How do you know that?"

"Because I feel the same, Mary." Only, Nicholas didn't say the rest of what lay in his pounding heart—that she enticed him as a man. He found himself wanting to kiss her mouth and discover the taste of her. Feeling out of kilter, he added softly, "But I am glad to be here with you. My duty is to protect you, and I will do that with my last, dying breath."

D0205858

Books by Lindsay McKenna

LINDSAY McKENNA

As a writer, Lindsay McKenna feels that telling a story allows her to share how she sees the world. Love is the greatest healer of all, and her stories are parables that underline this belief. Working with flower essences, another gentle healer, she devotes part of her life to the world of nature to help ease people's suffering. She knows that the right words can heal and that creation of a story can be catalytic to a person's life. And in some way she hopes that her books may educate and lift the reader in a positive manner. She can be reached at www.lindsaymckenna.com or www.medicinegarden.com.

LINDSAY
McKENNA

GUARDIAN

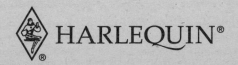

HARLEQUIN®

TORONTO • NEW YORK • LONDON
AMSTERDAM • PARIS • SYDNEY • HAMBURG
STOCKHOLM • ATHENS • TOKYO • MILAN • MADRID
PRAGUE • WARSAW • BUDAPEST • AUCKLAND

Recycling programs
for this product may
not exist in your area.

ISBN-13: 978-0-373-61836-1

GUARDIAN

Dear Reader,

When I was in the Museum of Gold in Lima, Peru, in 2000, I saw an incredible necklace beneath a glass case. It had golfball-sized emeralds, so clear that you swore you were looking through green glass. Below this stunning necklace was a sign that said it was found in the grave of an Inca.

I stood there stunned and began speculating. I wondered from which emerald mine the Incas had found these giant crystals. Who had transported them by foot back to Peru? They had to have been shown to an Incan emperor who, no doubt, ordered them cut, shaped to create a magnificent ceremonial necklace.

My mind raced until an idea for a series hit me. I called it *Warriors for the Light*. *Guardian* is the sixth and last book of this series. I hope the series has captivated you as much as it has me. Come visit me at www.lindsaymckenna.com. I always love to hear from you.

Warmly,

Lindsay McKenna

To Thomas J. Mitchell and his son Stuart Mitchell, composer. Thank you, Tommy, for all your incredible work with Rosslyn chapel and discovering the music encoded within the stone sculptures. Truly, your labor of love and patience has given our world healing music and resonation that can do nothing but lift the energy of the Earth.

ACKNOWLEDGMENT

Without the help of Thomas J. Mitchell, author of *Rosslyn Chapel, The Music of the Cubes,* 2006, and "The Roslyn Motet," by Thomas J. Mitchell and Stuart Mitchell, this book could not have the depth of information contained within it. And *The Woman with the Alabaster Jar* by Margaret Starbird. Her understanding of feminine symbols and biblical exploration were of immense help. Thank you, Margaret, for your wonderful discoveries.

And to Joke (Yokah), hostess of Les Labadoux, France. To Henry Lincoln, one of the authors of *Holy Blood, Holy Grail,* who helped me see things that were right in front of my eyes, but didn't see. And lastly, but never least, Ani Williams who shared her wealth of spiritual knowledge with pilgrimages to sacred sites around the world, thank you!

Chapter 1

Saint-Martin-Vésubie, 1308…

Fire!

Nicholas de Beaufort's heart beat as if it would lurch out of his chest. Fire and smoke! He tugged violently at the ropes binding his wrists. They cut deeply into his flesh but he didn't feel the pain as much as desperation to escape. He stood on a pyre of burning wood, bound with other Templar knights—all men of a loving Cathar God who promoted only compassion. Catholic priests, an army from Pope Innocent III and the French King

Phillipe III's soldiers taunted and cursed them. These were the men of the Albigensian crusade who had wiped out a million Cathars and the Templars in southern France. With a mighty roar, the flames from the outer edges of the stack of piled wood raced inward.

The chain mail Nicholas wore over his tunic absorbed the coming heat. Still, it wouldn't save him. Nostrils flaring, Nicholas tried to steady his fear. *Pray for their souls.* He had to pray! The other Templars, his brothers, prayed out loud for their rabid enemy. He had to be just as selfless and forgiving.

Smoke writhed between them. Nicholas choked and coughed. His eyes teared up from the constant smoke now cloying his lungs. *Dear God!* His mind wrenched from rage to terror. Pope Innocent III had ordered the Templars destroyed. His own leader, Jacques de Molay, was tied next to him.

"Courage!" de Molay shouted. "Courage! Pray for our enemy."

Blinking through his tears, his eyes smarting from the heat and smoke, Nicholas watched as the fire quickly ate its way toward them.

Saint-Martin-Vésubie, a small village in southeastern France, was attacked by the king's and Pope's soldiers. The surprise had worked. No Templar had known that they were suddenly the enemy of the King of France and the Pope of the Catholic church. For a year after their capture, they had been in prison. All had been dragged from their cells and tied at the stakes to be burned to death.

As Nicholas heard his friends, men with whom he'd fought, prayed, he envied their special courage. The heat rose and the wind fed the flames. His chain mail became so hot he could feel it scorching his skin.

He was going die!

Nicholas had long ago given up the resistance to death, for a Templar's life—and death—were built around the understanding that Heaven was waiting for them. Their reputation during the Crusades against the Infidels was that they would fight to the last man. Templars did not run. They fought and they died to bring Jerusalem back into the hands of Christians.

His eyes squeezed closed. The smoke choked him even more, and the fire licked at his booted feet. Despite everything, Nicholas tried to free himself, never mind that there were six hundred men on foot and on horseback surrounding the enormous funeral pyre that held the thirteen Templars.

Nicholas had just returned from the Crusades, injured badly enough that Grand Master de Molay had called him back to their headquarters in France. His days of fighting were done, Nicholas had been told. Now, he would work with the Grand Master on financial matters. The flames licked closer, and his feet began to burn. The pain soared up his legs. Nicholas groaned, clenched his teeth, and his head reared back against the rough-hewn log he was tied to.

The jeers and cries of their enemies crescendoed as the flames shot skyward. Nicholas felt the pain eating up his legs. His clothes caught fire. *Oh, God! Have mercy upon their souls….* He held on to that last thought as the smoke entered his lungs. He remembered the Templars, their high-minded focus, their reason for being: to protect travelers who wanted to make the long, arduous journey to Jerusalem to pray. His mind became unfocused. The smoke smothered his breath, stealing his oxygen. Just as a wall of flames exploded toward them, Nicholas lost consciousness.

Jerking awake, Nicholas breathed erratically. It took precious minutes to realize it was dawn at the Village of the Clouds. Sitting up on his pallet, naked except for a light blanket purling around his hips and lower body, he trembled outwardly. The nightmare. Always the same nightmare: burning at the stake in the village square with his Templar brothers.

Nicholas thrust himself to his feet. He stood naked in the thatched-roofed hut in the dawn light. Through the open window, the sun was a pink-and-gold ribbon on the horizon. Rubbing his sweaty face, Nicholas turned on his heel and strode out to the front of his hut where there was a table and chairs.

He grabbed a pottery water pitcher and filled a cup with shaking hands. The smell of smoke remained with him. He could hear the cries of his brother Templars. And the jeering and joy of their enemies—the king's and the Pope's soldiers—haunted him. Lifting the cup to his lips, Nicholas gulped down the tepid water. The cooling draft convinced him he was alive and no longer tangled in that horrible nightmare.

Trickles of water dripped down from the corners of his mouth and onto his bare chest. They felt life-giving—an affirmation that he wasn't trapped in that incarnation or that body. Pulling the mug away from his lips, he wiped his mouth with the back of his hand. He absorbed the simple lifestyle of the *Taqe,* the People of the Light, yet some moments, it took effort to control his escaped emotions.

As he had died in 1308, tied to that pole, his spirit had broken the silver cord between itself and the body of the French-born Templar he'd inhabited for twenty-eight years. The next thing Nicholas knew, he stood before a small wooden bridge across a trickling stream. Through fog, he heard someone walking across the bridge. It had been Alaria, the leader of the Village of the Clouds, who had met him. He was still stricken with grief and anger over the trauma of his death.

"Be at ease, my son," Alaria had said. She had reached out with her aged hand and placed it on his shoulder. "You are safe. You need not fear anymore."

Nicholas stared emptily at the beautiful dawn spreading its light across the many tilled fields at the slopes of the Andean mountain chain. In reality, they were in the fourth dimension, the Village set in Peru with the Andean mountains as their home. No one knew they existed. Few could see into the fourth dimension. The Village of the Clouds was the protected fortress and main headquarters for the *Taqe,* the People of the Light. Those who came from the heart, who tried their best to practice compassion, came here to rest and be schooled between lives.

Nicholas rubbed his chin. He took great care to have his beard trimmed and neat-looking, just as it had been when he had been a Templar. He had been given the chance to dissolve that personality when he'd walked across that bridge into the safety of the Village of the Clouds, but Nicholas had not. He was proud of that lifetime, of what he'd accomplished. His faith in a creator, no matter by what name, was deep. In his twenty-eight years of life back then, Nicholas had helped many. He'd been a Cathar Christian monk who had lived a life according to the Church of Love—from the heart. He'd worked hard all that life to remain in his heart and do the right thing for the right reasons.

He'd had many lifetimes as a warrior. Nicholas knew that killing was wrong, that war was wrong. He never wanted to give up his personality as a Templar knight and Cathar monk. No one here made him do otherwise. Those who lived here in the world of spirit could practice and believe as they wanted. Nicholas had a voracious desire to understand his tie with his loving God of boundless compassion. Grimacing, he padded back into the other room. His clothes lay neatly folded on a wooden shelf. He pulled a white long-sleeved shirt over his head. The brown cotton pants reached to his knees. He had found going barefoot was best.

In another hour, he would meet with other men and women from the village and go out to toil in the fields. This produced their food for a village of nearly one thousand people. He was proud of his ability to work all day in the hot sun. His body was strong and his desire to do the work to feed others gave him a sense of humility and accomplishment.

Nicholas just wished he could get rid of that one nightmare. Oh, he knew he had a choice. Alaria had counseled him that in order to work through the horror of being burned alive and betrayed, he'd have to go back into a human body. That he refused to do. Alaria had given him a sad look of understanding and said nothing more. The centuries had fled and Nicholas had watched with fascination as countries and continents won and lost everything. But he didn't want to go back there, back into another incarnation. It was just too much for him to deal with.

After brushing his teeth, he picked up a pair

of sharp scissors. As he looked at his sun-darkened face in the mirror, he noted a handsome man with a short black beard. The beard emphasized his large green eyes and thick black eyebrows. He saw the sword scar he carried on his right cheek. He'd gotten that in a fight to the death with a Saracen lord who had sworn to kill him. They'd fought—he with his long sword and dagger, and the Saracen with his curved scimitar. Nicholas combed his straight hair that pooled around his broad shoulders. Even in the dawn light, it gleamed with health and blue highlights. There was a sense of satisfaction even now as Nicholas remembered his dagger sinking through the armor the Saracen wore. The man had died an honorable, clean death. And Nicholas had prayed for the warrior's soul.

Finishing his toilette, Nicholas felt more emotionally stable. Alaria had told him that in the event of a traumatic and tragic death, a soul frequently would take five hundred to a thousand years of Earth time before it was ready to continue the incarnation cycle. Such trauma was horrifying and souls worked on such an experience to discharge the terror.

Nicholas snorted and looked around his quiet hut. He would never go back to Earth in an incarnation. Here there was a modicum of peace, of escape from the terrible deaths of humans. Yes, there was always the cursed nightmare, but he was willing to put up with it. Alaria had said it was his spirit trying to discharge the energy of that trauma, and it would, over time.

"Nicholas?"

He looked up to find Alaria in a peach-colored robe, standing in the doorway. He'd not heard her approach. "Mother," he said, smiling with welcome. He never saw her this early.

She tucked her hands into the long sleeves of her robe. Her silver hair fell in two long braids across her proud shoulders. "Something urgent has come to our attention. Can you meet Adaire and me at our hut?"

Frowning, Nicholas said, "Why, of course." He watched her nod and disappear. What was up? Had the Dark Lord, Victor Carancho Guerra, done something new? He was fighting the *Taqe* for all seven spheres of the Emerald Key Necklace. Whoever got it would hold sway over the energy on Earth. Either the heavy energy of the *Tupay* or the light energy of the *Taqe* could rule.

Taking another drink of water, Nicholas could have willed himself to the hut that lay at the entrance of the village, but he didn't. Nicholas loved exerting his physical form. He liked the sweat of working, the ache of his muscles after a long day's work out in the fields. He enjoyed bathing in the coolish stream, the scent of lavender soap against his sweaty, sunburned flesh. Yes, there were many luxuries from his Earth incarnations that he wanted to continue.

He left his hoe against his hut and padded down across the center of the village. Men and women were tending the many fires where blackened iron tripods held kettles of cereal to feed the hungry village. The scent of quinoa grain, a specialty of South America, entered his nostrils. It had a sweet, nutlike scent and tasted equally good when eaten.

Sleepy-eyed children stumbled out of the huts with parents behind them as they headed for the benches surrounding each tripod. Dogs barked and played farther away from the main breakfasting areas. Tropical birds called back and forth along with the howler monkeys that lived in the nearby jungle. It was a pleasant cacophony for Nicholas as he strode toward the largest hut in the center of all the bustle.

Above, the usual wispy clouds moved with slow-motion grace. The sun had not yet risen. The air was cool and felt good on his skin. This was a favorite time of day for Nicholas. As he moved closer and closer to the hut of the leaders of the *Taqe,* he wondered what had happened. He had not read any stress in Alaria's deeply lined face. But she never conveyed hardship of any kind. She had no more earthly incarnations left to live out, nor did her husband, Adaire. They had transcended such things, which was why they were the leaders of this wonderful, healing place.

Adaire, with his long silver beard and his hair around his shoulders, greeted Nicholas. Today, the Arch Druid of Mona wore a long gray tunic. A simple leather belt emphasized his height and wiry body. A smile touched Adaire's mouth.

"Welcome, my son. Come in."

Nicholas nodded. Stepping inside, he anchored himself. There, at the round wooden table, sat Alaria. But it was what was on the table that got his full attention. It was one of the emerald spheres that the *Taqe* had managed to find. The sphere, the size of a robin's egg, glowed green and gold. The flashes of light reminded him of lightning on a dark, stormy night.

"Ah," Nicholas said, bowing slightly to Alaria, "I had heard of these spheres but had never seen one until now."

Alaria nodded. She had put three wooden mugs filled with a lemony-scented herbal tea on the table. "Indeed, Nicholas. Come, sit down with us. Have you eaten yet?"

Adaire sat down and Nicholas followed. The wooden chairs were handmade and were beautifully carved and crafted. The seats were woven from strong, brown grass and sitting in them was always a pleasure. "No, Mother, I have not."

Adaire said, "We have already eaten. I can bring you a bowl of cereal from one of the tripods."

Touched that the Father of the *Taqe* would do this reminded Nicholas that they were leaders from the heart. There was no arrogance or sense of entitlement. In every respect, they mirrored his Cathar beliefs about living from and through one's heart. Their faces were deeply aged and full of kindness. Nicholas had heard they had been here since the fall of the island of Mona off Britain. Roman soldiers had crossed at low tide and they had slaughtered hundreds of druids— men, women and children. They had laid waste to the wonderful educational center that had supported all of Europe. Alaria and Adaire had died defending their island and their way of life. It had been their last human incarnation.

"No, thank you," Nicholas said, reaching for the mug of steaming herbal tea. "This will do." He put the mug to his lips and tasted the honey in the tea. He knew better than to speak, but felt no alarm.

"Nicholas," Alaria began softly, "we understand why you have chosen to remain here after your terrible demise."

Confused, Nicholas stared at her. "What are you asking of me?"

Adaire pointed to the glowing sphere. "Remember the legend of the Emerald Key Necklace, my son?"

"Yes. The Incan emperor, Pachacuti, sent seven of his priests and priestesses around the world to hide them. He knew that the spheres would be needed centuries later, when the world was in dire straits."

"Which it is right now," Alaria said.

"The legend is true, but it diverts a bit," Adaire said. "Legends add and lose information simply because the oral translation isn't always reliable. We still have two spheres to find. They are inscribed with *love* and *faith*. What has been lost from the legend is this—one Incan priest and priestess were married. They each had a sphere. They received permission from the emperor to place the last two spheres to-gether in one hiding place."

Brows rising, Nicholas murmured, "Well, that's good news, isn't it? All that needs to be done is to find the candidates, right?"

Alaria frowned. "Yes and no. The last two spheres have each selected a certain person to find them." She pointed to the fifth sphere in front of them. "We know that the spirit of the sphere will talk to that person in the dream world."

Still confused, Nicholas didn't understand why he had been summoned here. He'd had no dream, no calling of where the last two spheres were located. "All right," he said, his voice unsure.

Adaire patted his lower arm. "My son, we know from the spirit talking with us, that it has chosen a woman named Mary Anderson."

"She's human?"

"Yes," Alaria said. "She received the dream. We aren't allowed to ask the spirit anything by the rules of the Great Mother Goddess. But we can, if allowed, follow the energy of the dream to find out who has been selected."

"Well," Nicholas said brightly, "that's won-derful. Where is she?"

"She's an American," Adaire said. "She's a

quilting teacher and she's twenty-seven years old. Mary was on her way to Scotland, to Edinburgh, to give a series of classes on quilting to a quilter's guild. She had the dream while she was flying on a plane from New York City to London last night."

"That's great," he said. Thinking that they wanted to talk strategy with him, he found himself excited. The green glow that flashed around the hut was an amazing and wonderful energy. Every time Nicholas was bathed in it, he felt happy—and lighter. He itched to touch the sphere, but he knew better. If they offered it to him, that would be one thing. To touch a sacred object without permission just wasn't done. Nicholas kept his hands firmly wrapped around the wooden mug.

"It is," Alaria said. "From what the dream showed her, the spheres are located in Rosslyn Chapel." Her eyes narrowed speculatively upon Nicholas. "Does that ring a bell with you, my son?"

Nicholas straightened. "Yes, of course it does, Mother. Rosslyn is a Templar and Cathar chapel through and through. It was built in 1446 by Sir William St. Clair, who was a Templar himself. I was dead by that time, but I watched the remnants of the Templar knights scatter across Europe to hide from the Pope and his murdering Inquisition henchmen."

"Yes," Alaria said, "and there are certain ancient churches in Europe and the one in Scotland that create a powerful step-by-step process of spiritual development and advancement. Did you know that?"

Nicholas nodded. "I'm aware that there are six churches in Europe and Rosslyn Chapel in Scotland that symbolize the seven planets that were known by man at that time. And that Rosslyn was considered to be Saturn, the outermost planet discovered."

"And Saturn symbolizes physical manifestation in the third-dimensional world of Earth," Adaire added. "This chapel is where the two spheres are hidden. We are positive of that."

"We can't prove it," Alaria said, "but everything points in that direction, Nicholas. That is why we want you to incarnate back into the Earth plane and be a guardian and guide for Mary Anderson. You were a Templar knight. You know more about their secrets and symbolism than she ever will. She's going to need someone like you to help her find those last two spheres."

Nicholas reared upright, his mouth open. "What?"

Adaire eyed him grimly. "We need you to volunteer to go down there as a human, Nicholas. We can't make you go, but you are a Templar. The Dark Lord is furious that he didn't get this last sphere. He's willing to do anything to find the next one. He has no idea that two spheres are in hiding in one place. We need a warrior at Mary's side."

"We need you," Alaria said, her voice firm; she was not going to take no for an answer.

Chapter 2

Two green-and-gold eyes stared at Mary Anderson. She was sleeping at the Sofitel Hotel at the London Heathrow airport in England. She'd flown on British Airways from Phoenix, Arizona, to the UK. She was mesmerized by them; they reminded her of flawless emeralds with a thousand suns flashing within. They were surrounded by blackness. She tried to see the face that owned these two magical green eyes. Who was it?

Often in her active dreamworld at night, she would have several colorful dreams, but this one was different. Long ago, Mary had been able to enter her dream state. Her mother, Bridget, had said the women of her mother's family had lucid-dreaming ability. That meant she could wake up in the dream and become a more active participant within it. This time was no different.

Mary moved into the dream and found herself standing on an unseen dais. It felt like stone that had been cut and smoothed into blocks, tightly fitted against one another. The blackness did not scare her. Indeed, the energy around these two green eyes deluged her with wave after wave of love. She felt lifted, hopeful, and the energy trickled through her, making her feel joyful.

"Who are you?" she called. "May I see your face?"

There was no answer. In the background, however, she began to hear music—and voices. There was a sound of a harp, a woman's voice and then men joining in. If Mary didn't know better, she'd think she had been transported back to the Middle Ages and she stood in an unseen Gothic church listening to a choir singing. The music was beautiful, soft, and it began to surround her. She felt its movement like coils of energy softly moving around and around her.

"What do you want of me?" she asked.

The eyes began to flash more rapidly with the

gold light. And then, a powerful beam came from both green eyes and enveloped Mary. She was suddenly dizzy and closed her eyes.

In seconds, she felt movement around her, as if being transported. And then, the movement slowed and finally stopped. There was mist around her. As it dissipated, she saw a small, arched wooden bridge above a merry creek that bubbled happily beneath. She was aware of birds calling and singing. It was dawn and this place—wherever it was—welcomed a new day. The mist swirled and breathed as if alive. Mary sensed anticipation. She wasn't afraid, even though she was in an unknown jungle. The two green eyes had sent her here to have her question answered.

Mary became aware of a very old woman, her silver hair in braids over her shoulders, standing on the other side of the bridge. Her blue eyes were warm with welcome as she stood in a peach-colored robe. She wore sandals and her hands were hidden within the long sleeves. She smiled.

"I'm called Alaria, Mary. Welcome to the Village of the Clouds." She lifted her hand from within the fabric of the sleeves. "You are standing at the doorway to the *Taqe* or People of the

Light. We are a place where people of good heart come for training and learn to live compassionate lives."

Mary nodded and let the woman's wise gaze envelop her. More and more of the clouds dissipated, and farther up the well-trodden dirt trail she saw a village of many thatched huts. "I've never heard of this place," she admitted, curious.

Alaria placed her foot upon the bridge and walked across it to where Mary stood. "Many come here in their dreams and you have been here before, my child."

"Oh, I'd remember this place, Alaria. It's gorgeous. I would never forget coming here."

The energy of Alaria's aura surrounded Mary and she felt incredibly protected and loved. She knew this woman was not of her three-dimensional world.

"Ah, yes," Alaria murmured. "But some dreams are so deep within one's subconscious they are not remembered. That does not mean they don't occur."

Stymied, Mary looked past the tall, proud woman to the village in the distance. It sat at the foot of a massive mountain. Many people with hoes and rakes trooped out of the village and headed to the fields. "But," she protested lamely, "surely I'd remember this place."

Alaria gently placed her hand on Mary's shoulder. "My child, you come here often. You know our village well and have taken many courses in metaphysics with us over the span of your life."

Just the touch of Alaria's hand on her shoulder sent a wonderful warmth through Mary. She felt such a deep love of Alaria that it brought tears to her eyes. "But…surely I would remember you." She almost burst into tears, such was the intense love that moved between them.

"Be at peace, my child," Alaria said, allowing her hand to fall away. "From now on, you will recall your travels here."

"Why not before?" Mary self-consciously wiped the tears from her eyes.

"It wasn't time," Alaria said. "All things take time. And frankly, we had no idea who the emerald spheres had chosen to find them until you showed up here this morning."

Mary wanted to remember the Village of the Clouds. There was such peace and love within it that her heart cried out that she wanted to live here forever. "The emerald spheres?" she said, thinking back to the question in her dream. "Oh, you mean those two green eyes?" She saw Alaria's aged face glow and a smile wreathed her lips.

"Both came to you?"

"Yes…. I thought they were green eyes that belonged to a face I couldn't see. It was black, Alaria, and all I saw were the two green eyes looking at me."

"Ah, indeed. Well, this is good news."

Stymied, Mary asked, "It is?"

"Indeed. In the waning days of the mighty Inca empire, the last great emperor, Pachacuti, had a seven-strand emerald necklace produced. It was called the Emerald Key Necklace. He then sent seven of his best priestesses and priests to hide them around our globe. He knew that they would be found when Earth was at a critical juncture between the dark and light forces. People would be chosen who were Warriors for the Light, *Taqe* men and women who wore the Vesica Pisces symbol on the backs of their necks." Alaria motioned toward Mary's neck. "You carry this birthmark, my child. You are one of us."

Mary had been aware of the birthmark, but no one had known what it meant. "Do you know about this? All my life I have wondered what it meant. Clearly, it's a symbol."

Nodding, Alaria said, "This symbol is very ancient and was utilized by those who practiced geometry, from the Sumerians down through the ages. It is known as the womb or matrix of all geometric forms. It is shaped like an egg or seed and is associated with the sacred feminine within the ancient world. It was recognized as the Great Mother Goddess of us all. Those who carry this birthmark are from a special group of souls who know that the world must be balanced between the masculine and feminine. For the last two thousand years, Earth has been run by masculine energy only and it has allowed this imbalance to be ruled by the heavy energy of the *Tupay*. The Dark Lord of the *Tupay* revels in a world where the divine feminine has been completely suppressed by all religions."

Mary's birthmark throbbed and she rubbed it. "That must explain why I'm such an advocate of women's issues, especially with respect to leadership."

"Indeed it does," Alaria said. "Warriors for the Light want harmony on Earth. To have harmony, you cannot have a world run by one gender while suppressing the other. Only when the masculine and feminine work as a respected and equal team will the Earth move into the Light.

Until then, the solar masculine energy is driving the Earth deeply into the depths of heavy energy, which will eventually destroy it. When all seven emerald spheres are retrieved, we can have Ana, who is the daughter of the Dark Lord, wear it. She left her father's *Tupay* ways and now lives among us. In the legend it said the Daughter of Darkness would wear the Emerald Key Necklace and feminine energy would once more be restored to Earth. If this happens, it will be a great day for Earth and all her inhabitants."

"If? What do you mean?"

"Two spheres remain elusive. Our people have not gotten them yet," Alaria told her. "Those two green eyes you saw are the last two spheres."

"Oh, my," Mary said, realizing the enormity of Alaria's statement. "They aren't eyes. They are the stones from the necklace, then?"

"Exactly," Alaria said. "This means, Mary, that you were chosen by both spheres. You must find them."

"Do you know where they are?" Mary asked.

Alaria shook her head. "We think we know, but you must be told directly by the spheres. Move back into your dream state. See what they will tell you."

"And you will be watching and listening?"

"Yes, with your permission. We cannot do it without your consent, Mary. To simply push our way into your dreams is a *Tupay* activity. It is not something for people of the *Taqe,* or Light, to do. You are a partner here with all of us. You need to know about us and trust us."

"I do trust you," Mary whispered. She reached out and touched Alaria's shoulder. Instantly, a wave of love raced up her arm and encircled her heart.

"Wonderful," Alaria said. "I will send you back into your dream. We will connect with it and you. And then we'll see where it goes."

"And I'll be able to contact you again?"

"Oh, yes." Alaria drew out two long strands of red yarn from her pocket. She held them out toward Mary to look at. "Find yourself some red yarn, and now, child, all you have to do is this. Watch me and learn."

Enthralled, Mary stepped back as Alaria laid down the first strand of yarn and created a circle. Then, she created a second circle overlapping the first. To Mary, it looked exactly like her birthmark.

"Once you have created the two circles that overlap," Alaria explained to her, "you want to step into the center where the overlap occurs." She demonstrated. "This is the Vesica Pisces, or,

in Latin, what they call the fish's bladder. This
is the seed. The place of harmony where the
masculine represents one circle and the feminine, the other. Where they overlap, Mary, there
is harmony. When you awake from your dream
and buy the two lengths of red yarn, I want you
to do what I do. Watch…"

Alaria stepped into one side of the Vesica
Pisces. "Keep your knees soft, my child. Stand
relaxed in this. Then, close your eyes and wait.
Soon, you will feel a movement, a tug either
forward, back or from the left or right. You and
your aura are being rebalanced so that you are in
a healthy energetic state once more. If you do this
daily or after you've had emotional trauma, it will
heal you and make you feel better. Standing in this
'eye' as we call it, once a day, will give you more
energy and vigor. You will see the world through
more compassionate and loving eyes. Anyone can
do this. First, you want to rebalance yourself in
the eye. Then, I want you to either sit or lie down
within the eye. Move into an altered state and call
my name. I will then come to you while you are
in that meditation state and we will converse."

"This is an amazing thing," Mary whispered
in excitement.

Smiling, Alaria said, "Oh, indeed it is. It's a

gift from those ancient mathematicians who discovered the properties of the Vesica Pisces five thousand years ago. It is a gift to all who want to utilize its properties. Best of all, it is free and it can do no harm, only good, because it comes from the source of a balanced paradigm of female and male energy connected in equal relationship with one another."

Mary watched as Alaria stepped outside the eye.

"So people like me, the *Taqe,* or of the Light, want the feminine back so it can bring peace and harmony once more to Earth?"

"You have it in a nutshell, Mary. That is the mission of the Warriors for the Light. And I'm not surprised that the last two spheres chose you, a woman, to find them. This is in keeping with the Great Mother Goddess's plan to bring harmony to this planet. By taking this mission, one that you incarnated into this body for this lifetime, you have a chance to change the world for the better. You are a Warrior for the Light whether you know it or not. And no mission you take is going to be easy or simple. It will be fraught with danger. It is a life-or-death mission."

"What if I fail, Alaria?" Mary felt sudden fear over that possibility.

Alaria held up her hand. "My child, we are sending a partner to help you. He was a Templar knight, a man of impeccable integrity and honor. He, too, is a Warrior for the Light and bears the same birthmark on his neck. He knows of the feminine through Mary Magdalene of the Cathar Christian religion. Nicholas de Beaufort will meet you shortly. Together, you will search for these spheres. He is your protector, your knight who will keep the *Tupay* away from you."

Feeling a bit better, Mary said, "Thank you. Will I know him?"

"Yes, he will come and introduce himself to you, Mary. Now, go back into your dream. Let the spheres show you where they are hidden."

Without warning, Mary felt her eyes close. The sense of sudden movement occurred once again. And then, she was back with the two green, glowing eyes. Emboldened by the information given by Alaria, she said, "Show me where you are. I will come for you."

In an instant, the scene before her changed. She saw a Gothic church, a sign nearby that said Rosslyn. She was shown the interior of the church and that's when the singing began. The inside of the chapel contained thirteen stone arches from floor to ceiling. Mary took in her surroundings. The singers were in medieval dress, their musical instruments also from that time period. Their voices flooded the chapel and swelled. Mary was overwhelmed by the beautiful, loving energy that gathered and then moved like a tornado swirling. She didn't know what it meant, but burned it into her memory so that once she awakened, she would remember everything.

"Come to us…come to us…." the spheres chanted as the scene dissolved and, once more, Mary was looking at the two green eyes.

"I—I will," she promised them.

Just as suddenly as it had come, the dream disappeared. Mary awakened, sat up in her bed, her heart thumping loudly. She looked around the quiet hotel room and noticed that the clock read 3:00 a.m., the time when she always got her precognitive dreams, the ones that came true. Getting up, she turned on a light and grabbed her dream journal. She furiously scribbled everything she could recall. The information was too important to forget.

The last thing she put in her journal was the name of the warrior-knight who would be at her side: Nicholas de Beaufort. Who was he and was he of this world? Mary would often see ghosts—or what her mother called "discarnates," spirits trapped in the Earth dimension—around people or places. For some reason, these beings refused to move on to the Light or heaven. Mary sat on the edge of her bed feeling frustrated. She should have asked Alaria more questions.

After closing her journal, Mary went to the desk in her hotel suite. There, she found a book and a map of the United Kingdom. At 8:00 a.m. she would board her flight to Edinburgh. She turned to the section on Scotland and thumbed through some pictures.

There! She gasped, stopping on a page featuring the Gothic church. Rosslyn Chapel. And yes, just as in her dream, the chapel was near Edinburgh, where she was to give her quilting workshop. Mary felt a sense of destiny—her dreams had never been wrong. They had helped her navigate the twenty-seven years of her life, and she always trusted what she got.

Looking back at the Rosslyn Chapel picture, she read the caption beneath it. It had been built by William St. Clair in 1446 and was rumored to be Templar-built and full of mystical secrets. Many thought the Holy Grail was in the chapel, in the section where all the other St. Clairs had been buried over the centuries, the crypt.

Mary recalled what Alaria had said about Nicholas de Beaufort—he had been a Templar knight. Curiosity ribboned through her. She closed the book and went to her laptop. She needed to do some quick investigation of Rosslyn Chapel and the Templars. A sense of excitement raced through her as she searched for information.

Surely going to Edinburgh was part of a larger plan. Never in her wildest imaginings had Mary ever thought she'd be a part of something so great and important to the Earth. Mary...of all people. The Vesica Pisces birthmark had been a silent symbol that had finally spoken to her. She was destined for this moment.

As Mary read voraciously through the early-morning hours, she began to realize that this dream was a turning point. And this male stranger, Nicholas de Beaufort, was going to help her on this road. There was danger ahead. She could feel it, as if someone else were watching her, marking her efforts. Could anyone else enter her dreams as Alaria had? She noted that the *Tupay* would barge into a person's dreams without their permission. Was that why Alaria had assigned a brave and courageous Templar knight to come back to guard her?

For now, it was all a mighty cosmic puzzle.

She got up to shower and wash her hair, feeling grateful to be watched over by the *Taqe*. And by the mysterious Nicholas de Beaufort.

Excitement flowed through her and Mary actually felt giddy. Yes, Alaria was right—this was why she had been born into this lifetime. She had a mission, and all the pieces she had wondered about for so long had just come together. And what an answer it was!

Chapter 3

Nicholas gritted his teeth. It had been centuries since he had moved into a physical body, and the process was uncomfortable. Not only did the language, the customs and idioms of the twenty-first century have to be part and parcel of his human memory, the heaviness was hell. He'd forgotten how light he'd felt as a spiritual being in the fourth dimension. The transformation was triggered by Alaria and Adaire, who had the abilities to put him in a particular place and time in history. He was a mercenary, a glorified guard dog to this Mary Anderson.

Nicholas materialized in a glen or meadow just below Rosslyn Chapel on the hill above. The late-August morning was cool, the fog lying in silent strands across the meadow. Most of the slope was steep. He stood next to a very old horse chestnut tree just below the summit of the hill. A well-used dirt path was beside him. As he thrust his hand out, his fingers met the bark of the tree. It felt comforting and stabilizing while his mind whirled with conflicting information. Nicholas gasped several times, hungrily inhaling the cool Scottish air deeply into his lungs. The oxygen fed his recently materialized physical form. His chest rose and fell with great drafts of air.

Nicholas had conflicting feelings about being here. Seeing Mary Anderson had persuaded him. What was it about her that had moved his heart? He had no explanation. In the end, he'd agreed to come back to Earth to protect her from the *Tupay,* and specifically, the Dark Lord, Victor Carancho Guerra, who would stop at nothing to get these last two spheres.

Flexing his hand into a fist, Nicholas looked down. He wore sneakers, jeans and a short-sleeved green plaid shirt. For all intents and purposes, he fitted in. He yearned for his mighty two-bladed sword. Moving his hand unconsciously to the dark brown leather belt surrounding his waist, Nicholas wished he carried at least a dagger. None was there. He flexed his shoulders and tried to feel at home in this physical body.

According to the watch on his wrist, it was 8:00 a.m., and the sun was above the horizon. All was quiet except for the chirping of birds in the trees. Brightly colored flowers dotted the grassy glen here and there. Eyes narrowing, Nicholas stood within the treeline, his hand still on the trunk of the chestnut. *Rosslyn.* His heart surged with a sense of incredible joy. He recalled that the last Grand Master of the Templars had created plans for this last chapel on an energy grid of seven to be built. There she was in all her glory. The chapel had a wooden wall around part of it and the rest was a wrought-iron fence. The gray stone chapel was undergoing restoration.

For a moment Nicholas felt as if he were back in 1308 before his death. The Gothic lines of Rosslyn Chapel triggered powerful memories and emotions of his incarnation as a Templar knight. His feeling for a loving God, for his Cathar way of life, was still within him. He'd been a married Cathar monk who also wore the trappings of a knight. He'd guarded many a pilgrim traveling to beautiful Jerusalem to pray. It had been a worthy life. Nicholas did not like to kill, but he had. That was the dilemma. The Templars lived in two worlds: that of warrior and that of Cathar monk. The Ten Commandments said "Thou shalt not kill," and yet, as a warrior, he had taken lives. The loving God he knew preached compassion, forgiveness and a life led by the Golden Rule: Do unto others as you would have them do unto you.

Nicholas had always been torn between the two worlds he lived in. And he would pay, someday, for those lives he'd taken. At the Village of the Clouds he had received information about all the great religions of Earth. He'd discovered similarities between many religions. For example, his Golden Rule had appeared in Buddhism in 560 B.C.—"Hurt not others with that which pains yourself." And in Judaism, he'd often run into "Thou shalt love thy neighbor as thyself." When he'd warred against the Saracens, he'd even heard it from one of the prisoners he'd taken. The soldier, one night, had spoken at length with Nicholas about his beliefs. When Nicholas had mentioned the Golden Rule, the man had smiled and said, "Whatever is disagreeable to yourself, do not do unto others." Nicholas had discovered this quote had roots in Zoroastrianism in 600 B.C.

He had been glad to be called off the highway from Europe to Jerusalem by the Grand Master. The more he delved into the Muslim Sufi beliefs, the more he found parallels in his own Cathar Christianity. Oh, to be sure, they were not exact parallels, but enough so that Nicholas had lost his desire to fight and kill. Beneath all the great religions lay the same messages of love, forgiveness and helping one another. All of that had been put to the ultimate test in Nicholas's life, when he was cruelly tortured and then tied to a stake.

As he stood there watching the strands of fog breathing in and out of the glen, he found the ability to forgive his torturers and captors. Even as he had lost consciousness, he had uttered the words of forgiveness, which is what had allowed him entrance into the Village of the Clouds. He had transcended and moved to a higher level within his heart. As he moved from one foot to another, Nicholas worked to adjust to the terrific weight that now hung on him. Living in the flesh was not ideal, he decided. But it had to be done.

Why had he agreed to this mission? Nicholas

knew the possibility of the *Tupay* attacking was great. He would become a warrior once more. Although Alaria had told him that this was an opportunity to send love to the attacking *Tupay*. That would earn him another refined level of understanding the ultimate power of love in all worlds and dimensions. Nicholas rubbed his chin, feeling naked without the beard he'd worn as a Templar.

As the sun rose higher he appreciated the fields and textured squares of wheat and grain across the gently rolling hills south of the chapel. Turning, he gratefully absorbed Rosslyn as it glowed in the golden morning light. Truly, the chapel was a key in many ways for pilgrims who wished to transcend their human wounds to become spiritually better. Nicholas knew it was the last of seven stops for a pilgrim who wished for spiritual advancement. He'd seen his Grand Master work with astrologers, mystics, musicians and mathematicians as they'd formulated the masonry sculptures adorning this Gothic place of power and beauty.

Nicholas itched to go into the chapel and see it for himself. He'd seen the plans so long ago. And the Grand Master, shortly before they'd all been captured by the soldiers of the king and the

Pope, had sent the finished blueprints home with one of his most trusted knights.

Now Rosslyn was in front of him. Nicholas could feel the energy pulsing from the Gothic chapel. Her large gray stones gleamed in the sunlight on the eastern side. The flying buttresses on the east and west sides kept the chapel upright. The buttresses were like mighty ribs on the outside of the chapel itself, beautifully sculptured by the many hands of skilled masons.

Indeed, the Earl of St. Clair had done an excellent job. He had been a Templar knight himself, a Cathar by belief, and he'd taken the duty of creating this majestic Gothic chapel as the last of the seven steps to spiritual advancement. Nicholas ached to stand within the chapel but it was closed for the next hour.

Moving his hand to his back pocket, he felt for his wallet. He took it out and saw he had plenty of pound notes. And several credit cards in his name: Nicholas de Beaufort. In his other back pocket was his French passport. Opening it, he noted that he had been born in Toulouse, France. And he had been back in the twelfth century. Proud to be from Languedoc Providence, one of several places where it held the yearly festival of Mary Magdalene. Languedoc

was a province that had lived a different branch
of Christianity than the rest of Europe.

The Cathars refused to accept Christianity as
put forth by the bishops in the first counsel of
Nicaea in 400 A.D. The Templars lived among
the Cathars and accepted their unique view on
the Christian religion. They accepted the Church
of Love that the Cathars lived by. Theirs was a
loving God and service to others was important. Furthermore, women were equals and respected, unlike the Christian religion put forth
by Nicaea. Those women were brutally suppressed and far from equal to any man who
chose that particular branch of the Christian
religion. When the king and Pope came swoop-
ing down upon the province, they not only murdered a million Cathars in southern France, they
wiped out the Templars at the same time.

After putting his passport away, Nicholas
climbed the knoll and walked across the glen
toward the walled Rosslyn Chapel. A car had
gone by on the dirt road, and people had started
to move around. He had to meet Mary Anderson
at the chapel since he was supposed to forge a
connection with this woman. Nicholas knew her
whereabouts and could read her mind at will. It
was necessary to do this under the circum-

stances. He could feel her approach Rosslyn Chapel via a taxi from Edinburgh airport.

The dew-laden grass slapped at his shoes as he made his way to the chapel. By the time Nicholas had crossed the glen, the sun was warming up the land. He reached the entrance to the chapel, but no one had arrived yet. An asphalt path at the base of the walled area led up to an entrance point, which was still closed to tourists. Nicholas continued to scan the grounds when he noticed the approach of a black taxi. His heart began to pound as he recognized the woman emerging from the vehicle. Mary Anderson had a sweet smile and a soft voice as she paid the cabbie and then closed the door. Turning, she walked a few feet across the road and then stopped.

Their eyes met.

The breath caught in his throat. Nicholas was stunned by the beauty of her curious gaze. Her eyes were a large sparkling turquoise. Thick lashes as black as her short hair emphasized them even more. What rocked Nicholas more than anything was her aura. It was filled with silver and pink, denoting someone who lived a gentle, compassionate life in her heart. Her oval face was highlighted with ruddy cheeks, as if she were out of breath and had been running a long distance. Her lips were full and even, curving in a smile. The sight of her made him smile, too. The colorful quilted vest, pink T-shirt and long, flowing light green skirt only added to her joyful appearance. Nicholas began to understand why the spheres had chosen Mary Anderson. She was a gentle spirit who moved quietly through this hard, unforgiving world. Even more, Nicholas began to understand why Alaria and Adaire wanted him here to protect her. There was a vulnerability about Mary in keeping with the sparkling silver and pink of her aura. She was incapable of protecting herself, he realized. And how had she managed to get this far without her face looking scarred, intense or marked by life?

Nicholas could not move. He was that affected by Mary. With a quilted bag slung over her shoulder, she walked from the cab to the path that led toward the chapel entrance. Nicholas tried to get a handle on these new emotions. He *wanted* her. The sensation was startling, rooting and hot. His loins suddenly began to burn. He could not remember ever feeling this needy about a woman. Confused, he became afraid of his own traitorous body. As a Cathar monk, he did not have to abstain from the mysteries and wiles of a woman. He'd married Madeline, a beautiful Cathar woman, when he'd come home to Languedoc. He'd loved her deeply for the year that he was home before being imprisoned and then later, burned at the stake. But this was different. He could tell Mary would affect him on a deeper level.

She stopped at the wooden gate that showed the times Rosslyn Chapel was open to the public. Straining her gaze upward, above the wall, she saw the top half of the mighty chapel. That's when she saw the man just off the path watching her. He was tall and proud-looking, his face narrow, green eyes intense upon her. For whatever reason, Mary sensed he was a soldier. A warrior. He appeared as lean as a wary wolf on the prowl. She liked his high cheekbones, his wide mouth and straight black brows. His hair was military-short and his hands hung loosely at his sides. There was a sense of action about him, as if he were about to move, to protect her. She could pick up energy around a person, and this man had a powerful sense of duty. It had to be Nicholas de Beaufort.

As if beckoned by some invisible magnetic energy, Mary walked up to him. The closer she got to him, the more she saw just how beautiful his green eyes really were—the color of tree leaves in early spring, they had gold highlights along with huge black pupils. He had the stately look of an eagle. She managed a slight smile and halted a few feet in from him.

"I'm sorry to bother you," she said, "but are you Nicholas de Beaufort?"

The intense expression on his face suddenly changed as she said his name. In its place, she saw hunger in his eyes, much like that of a starved animal. The raw need disappeared as quickly as it had come. He assertively held out his lean, callused hand toward her.

"Yes, I'm Nicholas de Beaufort. You must be Mary Anderson."

Mary felt as if she were in some kind of crazy dream. Oh, she'd had many dreams come true, but to have this man standing in front of her, well, it shook her to the core. Only when she slid her damp hand into his strong, warm one, did her heart start skipping beats. "Y-yes, I'm Mary Anderson."

Nicholas smiled down into her unsure gaze. "This is real," he told her, gently squeezing her hand and then releasing it. "Not a figment of your imagination." For whatever wild, untrammeled reason, Mary touched him as a man. She was graceful and reminded him of a beautiful willow tree. Her breasts were small and her hips not that curvy, but her femininity screamed at him. It took everything Nicholas had to release her soft fingers.

Gulping, Mary took a step back. "Did you read my mind just now? About the craziness of my dreams becoming a reality here?"

He smiled a little in order to try and allay her fears. "I did," he said with a slight bow. Some of his Templar ways remained with him. Women were equals among them, and they always deserved his respect and admiration. After all, women bore children, something a man could never do. They might not be as strong physically as a man, but from what he had seen in that last lifetime, they were high-tensile steel when it came to another kind of strength. They were superior in handling emotional tests. "I only meant to make you feel comfortable and not so frightened of me."

The timbre of his voice was low and French. Melodic. Mary nodded and gulped. "I didn't know what to expect this morning. Alaria told me to be here at this time. I really didn't think anyone would show up, to be honest. I thought my dreams had taken a turn around the bend and I questioned them. And Alaria."

Holding up a hand, Nicholas said, "Alaria will understand your reactions. We have other, more important things to do while we work as a team." He noticed the Original Roslin Inn across the street and motioned toward it. "May I buy you breakfast, perhaps? We can get acquainted."

It seemed like the right thing to do, and Mary smiled. She hitched the large quilted bag a little higher on her right shoulder. "I'd like that. I left my hotel this morning and only had a cup of coffee. I'm starved." She wondered if he was reading her mind again. There was such clashing energy around Nicholas. It was easy for Mary to imagine him in chain mail, a white tunic with a red cross on his chest, along with a sword and shield. No question he was very much a knight out of the Middle Ages.

"May I?" Nicholas held out the palm of his hand toward her left elbow. One never touched a maiden without her consent. Old Templar and Cathar ways were coming back strongly to him now. Nicholas saw her eyes widen with surprise and then Mary gave him a warm smile.

"Of course. Thank you." As he slid his callused hand beneath her elbow, her skin tingled wildly. Her heart picked up in beat. He checked his long stride for her sake as he walked her across Chapel Close to the hotel. There were few people about, except for a few locals going into the hotel for breakfast. As they neared the gray stone entrance to the ancient three-story building, he could smell bacon frying. The scent made him dizzy. He was starving! In spirit, they ate energy food that took on the look of earthly food but was not. But in a physical body his stomach needed real food.

Happiness threaded through him as he eased Mary up the one stone step and pulled opened the heavy wooden door for her. She moved inside the carpeted hotel. The scent of eggs, toast and bacon surrounded Nicholas like a fragrance. He spotted a sign that pointed to a narrow hall to the left of the desk. No one was around so he guided Mary toward it. He tried to discern where all this happiness originated and could only conclude that it was from Mary's presence. Nicholas tried not to salivate like a wolf on the prowl as his fingers cupped her elbow. Her skin was soft yet firm. A woman's skin. Skin to be explored by his fingers. Abruptly, Nicholas stopped that line of thinking. But it was more than thinking. His loins ached and he had to sternly reminded himself he was down here on a mission to protect her. That was all.

A waitress seated them at the large window

that looked out across the village of Roslin. Mary was touched by Nicholas's actions as he pulled the chair out for her. After the waitress brought the menus, Mary took in the old-world charm of the hotel. The drapes were cream-colored and drawn back to allow natural light to flood the dining room. Each square table was covered with a clean white linen tablecloth. A small pot of wildflowers sat in the center of each with the salt, pepper and sugar bowl. There were only three other people in the dining room at this hour. All men. They looked like businessmen catching breakfast before going to their respective jobs.

"A lovely place," Mary said, opening the menu. She peered over at her companion and noticed the yearning expression on his face. "You look sad."

Mary's words touched Nicholas, and he was shaken by her ability to read him. "It brings back fond memories of my last lifetime, in the thirteenth and fourteenth centuries." No one was near to hear their conversation or he wouldn't have admitted it to her.

Mary set the menu aside, her eyes widening. "Really? You're from that time? You've never had any other incarnations?"

He shook his head and closed his menu. "No. I did not want to come back after that lifetime." He didn't want to speak of his horrendous death and the residual trauma.

The waitress came over and interrupted their conversation. Nicholas seemed to relish giving his choices, and Mary was amazed at all the food he ordered. He had a rasher of bacon, four eggs, oatmeal and four slices of toast. He seemed puzzled by orange juice and instead asked for a pot of strong black tea. Hiding her smile, she gave the waitress her order. Mary folded her hands beneath her chin and studied her new friend. Why did he have to be so dazzlingly handsome? She saw a thin scar down the side of his face. She wanted to ask him about it but decided not to. Mary had seen the turmoil in his green eyes when he mentioned his life as a Templar. There was great angst with that life and she didn't want to upset him.

"You must be hungry," she teased with a smile.

"Starving. I've not been in body for a long time and suddenly, food sounds incredibly good to me." He loved her warm smile and the understanding in her eyes. There was so much he wanted to know about Mary.

The waitress brought Mary coffee and gave

Nicholas his pot of tea along with a hefty white mug. As Mary placed a teaspoon of sugar into her coffee, she watched him deal with the dainty white teapot. He was awkward while lifting the small cap and nearly dropped it on the table. Nicholas was all thumbs. The row of different tea bags was packed tightly in a small white container. Eventually, his struggles yielded four bags of orange pekoe and pekoe tea. Surprised that he put all of them in the teapot, Mary realized he really did mean "strong black tea."

"Is that what you drank when you were a Templar?" she wondered, motioning to the teapot.

Nodding, Nicholas said, "Yes, I gained a taste for the black tea in Jerusalem. The Muslims had it brought from a faraway land. I found it to my liking."

"Amazing," Mary said, awed by him. Here she was sitting with a man from another realm. Somehow, he had been able to come into a human body to be here with her. "This whole thing…you…Rosslyn Chapel and the emeralds…it's like I'm living in an unfolding dream."

"I understand," Nicholas said. "There's no sense of anchoring. You merely float between realms."

Mary watched him intensely. "Exactly. How do you know that?"

"Because I feel the same, Mary." Only, Nicholas didn't say the rest of what lay in his pounding heart: that she enticed him as a man. He found himself wanting to kiss her mouth and discover the taste of her, his forbidden fruit. Nicholas yearned to surrender to his need for Mary in all ways. And yet, he dared not. First of all, she did not seem interested in him the way a woman would be if a man had caught her fancy. Somewhat relieved by that realization, Nicholas knew he must focus on their mission. He added softly, "But I am glad to be here with you. My duty is to protect you and I will do that with my last dying breath."

Chapter 4

At the *Tupay* castle, Jeff Anderson took time out from his vigorous training schedule to research how to read a person's aura. He wanted to go check on his grandchildren, a favorite pastime. Having died as an army Ranger on D-Day, he never got to see his family grow and expand.

As he sat in the meditation room of his small apartment, he closed his eyes and moved into an altered state. The focus of his interest was Mary Anderson, his granddaughter. He had always enjoyed following her life because she was highly creative and a quilter. Jeff's mother had been a quilter and this talent had moved through the generations of women in his family.

Even though he was in spirit, Jeff could direct his focus to the third-dimensional physical world known as Earth. All he had to do was picture Mary's sweet, vulnerable face and he would be there in an instant. This time, however, he was surprised. She was sitting with a man in a hotel restaurant. Jeff then recalled that she would be teaching in Edinburgh. He saw her drawing pictures from her billfold and opening them up to the man who sat opposite her. Jeff listened in.

"Nicholas, this is my family." Mary placed three color photos and one black and white in front of him, her index finger on the first. "This is my mom, Sally. My father, Ted. This is my grandfather, Jeff Anderson." She smiled over at him. "My grandfather was a real hero in World War Two. He posthumously received a silver star for his bravery on D-Day." She grimaced. "My grandmother, Faye, always talks so wonderfully about him. I'm sorry I never got to meet him. Grandma, who is an ace quilter, showed me a special quilt she'd made with black-and-white photos of her husband. She keeps it on the back of her couch. I hope someday to meet a man that I love the way she loved my grandfather."

Jeff's heart opened with such love for Mary that he felt dampness around the edges of his closed eyes. How he missed being with his wife Faye and seeing his grandchildren. Often the Dark Lord, Victor Carancho Guerra, told him he was too attached to his last incarnation. Because he'd died and been met by one of Victor's soldiers shortly after death, Jeff had been per- suaded into coming to the *Tupay* castle to live and be further educated. He'd already gone out on one mission with the Dark Lord, and he'd learned a lot from it. Victor wanted men who had been warriors in earthly incarnations to be his soldiers in the *Tupay* way of life.

Jeff watched and listened as Mary talked about her family—and about him. He began to take more notice of the stranger with Mary. Who was he? The tall man had short black hair and intense-looking green eyes. He might not have been so concerned had he not seen the Vesica Pisces symbol on the back of the man's neck. He was a Warrior for the Light! What the hell was he doing there with Mary? They were natural enemies to all *Tupay*. Worried now, Jeff ob- served his granddaughter more closely. That's when he saw something he'd missed. Mary's hair was short, and her T-shirt exposed her slender neck. Why hadn't he seen this before? She, too, had the Vesica Pisces symbol on the back of her neck!

Shocked, Jeff broke the energy connection, opened his eyes and sat up. Elbows on his thighs, chin resting against his clasped hands, he tried to figure out what was going on. No one in his family had had that symbol on their neck. Why did Mary have it? Anxious, Jeff realized that symbol put Mary in jeopardy with the *Tupay* soldiers and, even worse, the knights, who stalked and killed Warriors for the Light. The Dark Lord had a standing order to kill outright anyone who bore the symbol.

Sitting up, he felt his stomach churn. What to do? Jeff paced his small meditation room in a quandary. His granddaughter was a hated *Taqe*. If Victor ever found out, Mary's life would be endangered. And no way did he want any member of his family murdered by the *Tupay* knights. He couldn't understand why Mary carried the birthmark.

He realized that Sally Langdon-Anderson, Mary's mother, might be a carrier of the *Taqe* birthmark. It certainly did not run in the Anderson family. Groaning, Jeff stopped. He had to find out what was going on. This time as he sat down he moved into secret stealth mode. This was a higher altered state of consciousness that usually guaranteed his going undetected. However, he knew from the last mission that *Taqe* were highly sensitive to the slightest energetic disturbance. Jeff worked very hard to disguise himself so he would not be found.

"Tell me about your dream," Nicholas was saying, sipping his tea. The waitress had just brought their breakfasts. He was starving, but he forced himself to eat slowly.

Mary told him about the two green eyes in her dream between bites of her breakfast. When she was done, she said, "And then Alaria informed me what they were."

Nicholas nodded, savoring the bacon in his mouth. It was greasy and salty and delicious to his awakening earth senses. When in spirit, they tasted food, too, but not like this. The flavors were far more intense. He repeated what Alaria had said about the legend of the Incan Emerald Key Necklace. By the time he was finished with a longer version of the explanation for her benefit, he'd wolfed down the huge breakfast. The strong black tea was a perfect finish to his first earth meal.

Mary thanked the waitress who picked up

their plates after they'd finished eating. She turned her attention back to Nicholas. "So, these last two were supposed to go to two different locations but didn't?"

"Correct," Nicholas murmured. He felt a presence. An invisible one. Who was lurking around them? There were now four patrons in the hotel for the breakfast hour. Switching to his clairvoyant senses, he sensed something nearby, but the unknown presence didn't feel threatening. Nicholas wondered if Mary, by talking about her lost grandfather, had brought his spirit to her. That could happen quite easily. Because he felt no threat, Nicholas focused back on Mary. He sensed the invisible spirit had great love for Mary.

"Why did they send you along? Alaria said this would be dangerous. She said you'd explain more about that," Mary said.

Nicholas sat back with his hands around the white mug of tea. She was so easy to look at. He could see why Alaria chose someone like himself to protect Mary. She was highly vulnerable and, despite her age, truly innocent to the ways of some Earth people. She lived in a compassionate way. She came from her heart and there wasn't a mean bone in her body. She lived just as the Cathars of southern France had lived. He wondered obliquely if Mary had had a lifetime as a Cathar in France. Nicholas had failed to look through the Akashic Records, which kept information on each incarnation of an individual. Her demeanor told him it was very possible.

"The Dark Lord, Victor Carancho Guerra, is ruler of the *Tupay*," he explained to her. "These are people with heavy energy. They are trapped by their darker emotions like hatred, anger, greed, jealousy and so on." Opening his hand, he added, "Guerra is energetically in charge of this Earth right now. The *Taqe* and the Warriors for the Light are trying to wrest it from him in order to help people down here."

"How do you help them?" Mary wondered, fascinated by his story—and him. She found herself wondering what it would be like to be touched by him. Her elbow still tingled from where his hand had rested.

"The Emerald Key Necklace is one of several artifacts designed to help all beings to move to the light energy. If people receive the release of this special healing energy, it will allow them to surrender their heavy energy and become lighter. As we make a choice to try and live in our heart chakra, practice compassion, it will stop the warring and killing here on Earth. Eventually, peace will come to this planet, which is the ultimate goal of the *Taqe*."

"How wonderful," Mary said, her voice wistful. "I hate that a war robbed me of my Grandfather Anderson. I don't believe war is the way to settle anything. We have to, as a race, learn to talk out our differences."

"Spoken like a true *Taqe*," Nicholas said with a slight smile.

"And yet, you're a Warrior for the Light," Mary said. "You have killed, too."

"We protect and defend, Mary. That is the major difference between us and the *Tupay* knights. We never initiate aggression. We merely respond to the attack. The *Tupay* practice aggression. They don't care if they murder someone. To them, life is cheap."

"And so," she said, trying to get the big picture, "*Tupay* knights and *Taqe* Warriors for the Light endlessly battle one another?"

"They have for the last five thousand years," Nicholas told her. "When males began to denigrate the Great Mother Goddess, to attack the feminine and suppress women, Earth was sent out of harmony. At that time hordes from the north swept down across Sumeria and turned a culture that had had equality between men and women to what it is to this day. Until recently, the *Tupay* held women down and kept them as secondary citizens."

Mary grimaced. "How will this finally change?"

"If we get the Emerald Key spheres, it will bring about the harmony we're all seeking," Nicholas promised her. "That is why this mission is so important. The *Tupay* will be on to us shortly. They've been able to pick up on this energy, find the people on the mission and then try to steal the sphere."

"Have the *Tupay* hurt anyone?" Mary wondered.

"Yes, one man on a mission was killed. And each team member chosen to find the next sphere has been attacked by the Dark Lord himself."

Suddenly, Mary didn't feel as hopeful. "They killed a man?"

"Yes." Nicholas saw the worry in her eyes. Without thinking, he reached out and touched her hand. "That's why I'm here, Mary. I'm your guardian. I am not afraid of the Dark Lord nor of any of his knights. I will protect and defend you with my last breath. You are safe with me."

His roughened hand was warm and comforting. As Mary connected with his gaze, she felt protected for the first time. His eyes were no longer hard and unreadable. They showed his vulnerability and the sight took her breath way. There was so much more to him than she'd first realized. Almost sorry when he removed his hand from hers, she managed a soft smile. "I believe you, Nicholas. Thank you for being here, for volunteering to take this mission." She looked around the atmospheric restaurant. "I love my life. I enjoy everything I do. I take nothing for granted because someday, I know I will be gone."

"Life is precious," Nicholas said, agreeing with her. While he ached for more contact, he tried to hide his shock over his unthinking response to Mary's worry. He'd reached out and touched her. Oh, sweet, loving God, she felt good beneath his fingertips! Her flesh was warm, firm, and yet, like soft silk. His hungry fingers wanted to explore Mary intimately. He made the mistake of looking at those beautifully shaped lips. Groaning inwardly, Nicholas realized she was now his Achilles heel. Of all things! He grew hungry for her, but didn't dare voice his deepest wishes.

* * *

Jeff didn't know how to deal with the shock. His granddaughter had been chosen to find the last two emerald spheres! Real fear raced through him as he leaped to his feet. The adrenaline rush was so powerful he gasped for breath. His stomach knotted into a hard rock of nearly unbearable pain. Worst of all, Jeff knew without a doubt that someone, a knight in the *Tupay* order, would find out about this, and then, Mary, his beloved granddaughter, would be hunted down and killed.

Wiping his mouth, he tried to think clearly. He was a *Tupay*. And yet, he wanted to find a way to protect Mary from his own kind. Once the Dark Lord discovered that she had been given the dream where two spheres were located, Victor would leap upon this with a glee that would send waves of energy across the land of the *Tupay*. All Victor wanted was more of the spheres. He had stolen one and he wanted the rest to ensure that the *Taqe* could never string that necklace together so that his daughter, Ana, could wear it to make the energy shift on Earth.

Opening the door, Jeff hurried out into his apartment. He was afraid. Afraid for Mary. For his family. Without thinking, he rubbed the back of his neck. He didn't carry the Vesica Pisces birthmark. Of course, anyone who carried the mark would be banned from the *Tupay* sanctuary.

As he looked out the window, he could see the castle turrets in the distance. That was where the Dark Lord had his office and where he hid the emerald sphere. My God, Guerra would eventually find Mary.

Where did that leave him? Ever since he'd accidentally touched the green aura from the last sphere, Jeff had felt different. Oh, he'd gone in for lab tests to ensure he had not been turned into a *Taqe*. Because, as Guerra had told him afterward, any *Tupay* touching that loving green energy would turn. And if he did, Guerra would destroy his soul, once and for all.

These thoughts collided in his mind as an icy coldness flooded his body. He'd never felt this before. What was it? When it reached his heart, he felt a violent shaft of white energy explode through his head and zigzag down through his heart. It knocked him unconscious. Minutes later, after coming to, Jeff sat up and found himself on the floor of his kitchen. Dazed, his mind shorting out, he wondered what had just happened. He felt different. Very different. And what had happened to the coldness stealing like a thief up through his body? Jeff placed his hand on his head. He felt no pain, just a sense of space…incredible space…and it was new to him.

He crawled to his feet and held on to the counter. Shaking his head, he found it impossible to push away the sense of expansion. Was his head larger than before? He touched his skull with his fingers, feeling around it. No, same head. Same size. So then, what was this sensation all about?

Trickles of peace and joy filtered through him. These were new, too. Should he go to the metaphysical clinic and get checked out? They'd know, wouldn't they? Intuition strongly cautioned him against going to the clinic. Whatever had happened, the *Tupay* wouldn't approve, Jeff sensed. And that was another thing: he felt incredible love radiating from his heart like huge waves produced by an ocean tide. The feelings were good, uplifting and fulfilling him in a way he'd never experienced before.

Jeff tried to understand the bizarre experience. He could only sense that a cosmic lightning bolt had appeared through the apartment roof and struck him. That awful iciness had been replaced by well-being, warmth, love. Jeff hadn't felt this way since dying and moving into spirit.

Exhausted, he went to his bedroom. Maybe if he took a short nap, this new energy would level off. The bed sure felt good to him as he laid his head on the pillow. In moments, he went to sleep. His last thoughts centered on his granddaughter, Mary Anderson, who was now in danger. Jeff hadn't prayed in a long time, but now, he sent out pleas and wishes to anyone and everyone who could help. Above all, he didn't want his granddaughter murdered by Guerra. The Dark Lord would stoop to any level to retrieve those last two emerald spheres. Anything.

Chapter 5

"I don't know what to do next," Mary admitted to Nicholas as they prepared to leave the restaurant. "Do you?"

Nicholas left money on the table and stood as Mary slid out of the seat. "I think we should go over to Rosslyn Chapel and snoop around. Perhaps we should take an official tour?" He looked at the watch on his wrist. They had only a few minutes to wait till the chapel opened.

"Sounds like a plan to me." Mary pulled the quilted bag across her shoulder and led the way out of the hotel restaurant. The sky was a light blue with a few puffy white clouds in the east. Outside, she shifted as Nicholas came to her side. She grinned as she heard robins singing. "I love it here. There's such peace."

The village of Roslin had been created by masons who had worked thirty-eight years on the construction of the nearby chapel. The highest buildings had three stories and the structures were made of hand-hewn stone blocks. Each building was connected to the next so that a block of buildings had no alleys.

Nicholas placed his hand beneath her elbow once more, telling himself he was just being a courtly knight. "There are a number of benches in place on the east and west sides of the chapel. After we pay our admission fee, let's go over there and sit down. We can get a sense of the energy and remain inconspicuous while we await the tour."

The traffic was picking up through rural Roslin. They walked down the narrow Chapel Close, a black asphalt lane roughly a quarter of a mile long, between the main area of Roslin village and Rosslyn Chapel. By the time they arrived, the walled wooden gate was open and visitors were being guided through the gift shop to pay their fee.

Once through the small shop, Mary sat down on the bench with Nicholas, who maintained a reasonable distance between them. He was always alert, his gaze missing nothing and no one. An old lady hobbling by got his attention as much as a tourist snapping pictures. Folding her hands, Mary waited.

The energy around Rosslyn Chapel was significant. Mary wanted to share this with her guardian but kept quiet. She sensed Nicholas would let her in on some secrets about this mystical place.

He placed his arm along the back of the wooden bench, his fingers nearly touching Mary's shoulder. Nicholas kept his voice low. "What I have to say is privileged information only for you, Mary. I don't know where the two emerald spheres are located. They could be inside the chapel or on the surrounding grounds. Have you had more dreams to indicate their whereabouts?"

"No," Mary said. His brow furrowed and his eyes became more intense. Nothing but warmth and a sense of protection emanated from Nicholas.

"When Pope Innocent III and King Phillipe of France destroyed the order of Templars, many of my brothers escaped beforehand. They fled to different parts of Europe. There were seven ships that made their way to sea before the Grand

Master was imprisoned. Some headed for England or other countries where they could not be found and persecuted. Each ship arrived safely and because the murder of our members was ongoing, the Templar knights moved quietly into the local populations and disappeared. They never told anyone that they were Templars. They changed their names and started all over." Nicholas gestured around the area with his hand. "A group of Templars settled here in Scotland. The Earl of St. Clair was one of the offspring of our knights. He had been an earl in France before the destruction of our order began."

"But, you said you were killed. How could you know all this?"

"There is a place called the Hall of the Akashic Records. It's an enormous temple located in the fourth dimension. It houses records of every incarnation, each lifetime, your thoughts, words and actions. Like a color movie, it shows your entire life, the people you met and your experiences," Nicholas told her. "I could go there and keep tabs on my friends who escaped. And, because I was at the Village of the Clouds, I was taught how to move into an altered state and actually visit Earth as a spirit. I could remain invisible and yet hear and observe what was going on with my friends who managed to stay alive after our destruction. I watched them live good lives and die. I watched their children grow, marry and have families."

"That's fascinating," Mary said, amazed by it all. "I never realized so much was available to us in spirit."

"It is available to anyone here on Earth, too," Nicholas said. "However, they have to be a *Taqe* or working toward being of the Light for access to the Hall of the Akashic Records. No *Tupay* is ever allowed within those hallowed doors. They would use such information against a person and that is breaking a fundamental cosmic law."

Mary pointed to the chapel. "And so, the William St. Clair who built this was an offspring of one of the original Templar knights who escaped from France to live here?"

"Yes. And this earl who was of Templar blood had been educated into the depths of our mystical traditions. That knowledge came from the original Templars and it was passed down through the generations unsullied and unchanged. William St. Clair knew exactly what he was doing when he built Rosslyn. It is based upon Jacques de Molay's drawings. When we go into this chapel, you are going to see symbols from the pre-Christian era, astrology, numerology, sacred geometry, religion and mysticism."

"How did he get away with all those things during the Dark Ages? I thought during that time the Catholic Church sentenced to death anyone who didn't believe the church line."

Nicholas smiled. "That's all true. The Earl of Rosslyn took a huge risk, but it was in his blood as a Templar to tell the truth that eventually paved the way for Rosslyn Chapel. And the truth is all we'll ever have, Mary. What St. Clair did was place the mystical codes from the Egyptian mystery schools into stone within the chapel. It is a spiritual road map for those with the right eyes. I know, because I watched the forty years it took to build this chapel. St. Clair remained true to his vision and the metaphysical truths. One day, he knew, the right person would come along to decode what he'd had his masons create in stone within this chapel. He left a trail of crumbs, so to speak, to those who could see beyond the prettiness of the stone sculptures within it."

"Did the earl have a vision like I did?"

Giving her a slight smile, Nicholas nodded. "Yes, this particular earl had great metaphysical talents. He was an adept, a trained metaphysician in all respects. And his talent was inherited from the original earl who escaped France and came here to Scotland. All Templars were mystics but that information was historically suppressed by the Pope and the king. Who we were was destroyed to a great degree, but not entirely. All of this isn't known to modern-day history unless you start digging and asking questions. Some of us were adepts, followers of the ancient Egyptian mystery school that transcends time and cultures. There are mystical truths that will always be truths no matter what label you put on them, or what culture or group claims them for their own. Some things in our cosmos are sacred and given to all those who want to connect spiritually with that particular symbolic energy. And in connecting, one's soul is set free to evolve more rapidly and find union, once more, with the Light."

"The Templars were way ahead of their time," Mary noted. "They knew too much and it sounds like the church got scared of them." She regarded Nicholas with newfound respect. Not that she didn't like him anyway. When she looked into his green eyes, they had such depth and clarity that she felt surrounded by the energy of his passion for the Templars. Their job was to try to lift the world's energy to a better place. Her heart opened and Mary was powerfully drawn to this enigmatic knight-monk. There was a sense of danger about Nicholas but she could sense the kindness in him, too.

"That is true," Nicholas murmured. "When a man—or woman—volunteered to become a Templar, he or she gave his word on his life not to reveal the mystical information he received."

"Tell me more about the Templar agenda," Mary asked.

"We were an attempt by the *Taqe,* the People of the Light, to bring hidden mysteries and information back out into the world, where it belonged. The Romans destroyed the mystery school at Alexandria, Egypt. When it went up in flames, all the knowledge was lost. Then, the religions called this knowledge pagan and, therefore, wrong. Metaphysical truths are never wrong, Mary, but the men in power who control Christian religion made the people believe that." Nicholas removed his hand and sat against the bench, hands folded in his lap.

"What a loss to all of us, then," Mary said, saddened.

"And because the Templars had found hidden

documents that had been secreted away before Alexandria was destroyed, we brought them back to Europe with us. These mystical texts set the Templars on a course of destruction with the Pope, and he became wary of us. Not only that, the Templar order had amassed great fortunes of money over time. We were a powerful group and I feel that those two things were our downfall."

"But did you openly practice your mystical ways? I've never read anything about the Templars that suggested such a thing. All I know is that the Templars had secrets but no one outside the organization knew what they were."

He shrugged, remembering that day so long ago. "That's correct. Once a man or woman took the Templar promise, the mystical information we had was never shared outside our organization. There were other things that caused the Pope to fear us, however. The Cathar people not only grew in population to over a million people in southern France, but they believed that each person could have a personal connection with God. The Catholic church, of course, did not. They wanted people to believe that a priest must intercede on their behalf with God. The Cathars treated women as equals, the Catholic church did not. The Cathars called their church the

Church of Love. They had a God and Goddess who loved them, the Catholic church did not— they had a God that you feared. The Cathars believed in humility and service to others and to the village."

Mary nodded. "Huge differences."

"Yes. The Pope and the Catholic church wanted to control and disempower the growing Cathar population of France. He was afraid that Cathar beliefs and their way of living would erode his take on Christianity. King Phillipe wanted our money from our coffers and our extensive land holdings."

"I never knew all of this," Mary admitted. "You had the Pope after you for one reason, and the king for another."

Nicholas chuckled a little. "The king never found our money. We had hidden our gold and treasures in various places in the Middle East, in Jerusalem and in different caves or castles throughout Europe. Our Grand Master always followed this tradition. That way, if our order was ever raided, our enemies would never find much of value. He had made plans long before disaster struck."

"Wow," Mary said. "That's an incredible story. Talk about rearranging history and what we know about the Templars and Christianity. So, what if someone from today stumbled upon it?"

Nicholas saw a few more people lining up at the admissions office outside the chapel. They had ten minutes before the tour began. "Actually, one Catholic priest did stumble upon some of it. The Grand Master had hidden money in some of the caves beneath Rennes-la-Château in Languedoc, the home of the Cathars. Father Bernager Sauniere found a Templar map and located the cache in the early 1900s. Of course, he never said what he found or how much he found, but it would be worth several million dollars in today's world."

"And what did he do with the money?" Mary asked.

"He built an abbey to honor Mary Magdalene, fed the people of Provence and helped the poor. The villagers dearly loved this priest. Eventually, the Pope took away his priesthood and got rid of him. But, he continued, with our treasure, to help others until the day he died. That was our goal—always to help others."

"Was Father Sauniere really a Cathar in disguise?" Mary asked.

"I believe so. He certainly lived by their beliefs

and had a profound knowledge of Mary Magdalene, which is all part of the Cathar traditions."

"It breaks my heart that the Pope and the king murdered all of you."

It was an innocent and beautiful sentiment. Nicholas could see she meant it by the confusion in her huge blue eyes. It was easy to look at her and he found himself taking every opportunity to do so. What would it be like to kiss those soft lips of hers? The thought made him dizzy, and he clamped down strongly on his desire. "They feared us. They knew we had secrets that we wouldn't share with them. And even if we had, they would have rejected the Cathar Christian knowledge out of hand because it didn't fit conveniently into their concept of what they wanted the people to believe. So long as all women were suppressed, the church had the upper hand and control."

"You must have felt betrayed."

Flexing his long, narrow hands, he stared down at them for a moment. "It took me a long time to forgive them for what they did to us. As Templars we were slowly lifting the world out of the mire of darkness that the Pope had plunged the world into. Shortly after our destruction, the Renaissance came into being," he said with the barest of smiles. "In one way, we did help science and art flourish once more. The Grand Master had contacted men and women from the Middle East and Europe and given them back this mystical information. Artists and authors began to encode their messages into their works of art and books." Nicholas stood and offered his hand to her. "The truth is out there in paintings by many of the masters, including Da Vinci. There are documents in existence that are encoded. If a person wants to discover the truth, it is there for the taking. Are you ready to enter our realm?"

"Indeed I am!" She eagerly took his extended hand. As Mary got to her feet, she saw his large eyes change and become more feral. In that instant, Mary understood that Nicholas wanted her. It was a thrilling discovery, but she wasn't sure what to do about it. Her own past washed across her and she gently pushed aside the desire for him. They had more important work to accomplish, so she set her mind to it.

But Mary wasn't prepared for the energy within the chapel itself. They were the last of eight people who followed a highly knowledgeable staff person through the west door. The energy was powerful and struck her as combined male and female energy, or what was known as androgyny, the most perfectly balanced and harmonious of all energies. Nicholas maintained his cupped hand beneath her elbow, a gesture she found reassuring and touching. As she looked around, she was transfixed by what she saw.

The entire chapel contained hundreds of stone carvings. The group moved forward down the center aisle, the wooden pews in rows on either side of them. What drew her were the thirteen stone arches. They reminded her of ribs and, indeed, these massive stone arches provided a key role in keeping the chapel from collapsing in on itself. Her gaze fixed upon the hand-hewn stone "cubes," as Nicholas referred to them. There were at least thirteen cubes, carved and placed like hanging decorations on each of the arches.

When they got to the eastern end of the incredible chapel, Mary gazed up at the cubes, her brow knitted. In a low voice, she said to Nicholas, "Look at these. There has to be something about them. Why would the earl have all these made if it wasn't some kind of symbol or code sitting there staring back at us?"

"Precisely," Nicholas whispered back. "One man, Thomas J. Mitchell, thought that very thing.

He spent twenty years decoding these cubes," he said, motioning above his head at them. "And then they gathered an orchestra and a choir utilizing medieval instruments and created a CD of music. That music is healing. And he also wrote a book called *Rosslyn: Music of the Cubes*. We owe him much," Nicholas told her.

Mary felt a jolt of power as they passed by stairs leading down to where the vaults had been at one time. The vaults had held the bones of all the St. Clairs and Sinclairs. She hesitated. The group continued on around the chapel, but she stopped. There was a set of steep stone stairs that led down to a rectangular black stone floor below. She wanted to follow this incredible energy. Nicholas came to her side.

"That's the crypt," he told her.

Mary noticed they'd been left behind by the crowd. "Come on," she urged, taking his hand and pulling him along. "We'll talk about this crypt later."

As soon as they caught up with the group, she released his hand, but she didn't want to. His eyes had warmed as she'd reached out for his hand and gripped it. A mild electrical shock had traveled through her hand as she'd held his. What kind of power did Nicholas possess? Mary knew he was a big cosmic guard dog to her, but she had little real understanding of this unique human being. And she wanted to know much more.

Once again, they were outside the chapel. They toured the manicured grounds and went back to the east side where the grave headstones were located. Through the friendly guides, Mary found out a lot more about the history of this incredible chapel. Some of it, however, did not jibe with what Nicholas had shared with her. The guides couldn't know some of the information but what they did know impressed the curious tourists. She and Nicholas walked back to their bench and sat down. The warmth of the sun felt good.

"So? What did you sense?" Nicholas asked her. He wanted to move closer to her but didn't dare.

Shrugging, Mary said, "I didn't get anything about the spheres, if that's what you're asking."

"The energy in there is unique and different depending upon where you are standing. What you were feeling was sacred geometry in motion. The Temple of Solomon was created on mystical mathematics. When his temple was destroyed, the knowledge was carried forward by master masons, and it is known as geometry.

The Freemasons are the modern-day holders of that information. A series of churches in Europe were built with these mystical proportions, the Golden Ratio. For example, the Greek Parthenon was created using this mathematical equation. Rosslyn was built upon this mystical mathematical information, as well."

"I don't know anything about sacred geometry," Mary admitted. "Mathematics comes into play with quilting, but I don't think it's the same thing." She smiled.

"Sacred geometry, to keep it very simple," Nicholas told her, "is mathematics that is common in art and architecture. It mirrors the laws of resonance, the earth energies and cosmic energies around us. With geometry and the Golden Ratio, these energies can be focused, collected and placed into structures such as Rosslyn. The stone masons under St. Clair's guidance created a resonance that holds, like a woman's womb, not only the powerful energies of our mother, the Earth, but also the energies radiating from the Great Mother Goddess. They are held here in stone according to mathematics, and anyone walking into such a place will feel them."

"I sure did," Mary said, excited. "I felt uplifted, lighter, happier and I felt like singing!"

Smiling, Nicholas murmured, "There is a parallel between sacred geometry and the diatonic scale of music. Did you know that?"

"No, I didn't."

"You saw all the angles in Mary's Chapel in there holding medieval musical instruments?"

"Yes. They were everywhere. I haven't been in many Gothic churches. I was struck that they might have been carved in there to encourage music and singing here at Rosslyn."

"You're very good," Nicholas praised. "The diatonic scale which you know as do, re, me, fa, so, lah, ti, doh, is reflected in stone. Your desire to sing shows your sensitivity to what St. Clair put in stone for all who visit this very special chapel."

"Why did St. Clair do that?" Mary asked, frowning.

"Music…" Nicholas sounded wistful. He focused and looked over at her. Once more, she looked serious. "Have you ever heard of the music of the spheres?"

"No."

"It is the Great Mother Goddess's music," he told her. "If you are of sufficient evolvement from a soul perspective, you can hear the music. It is all instrumental and beautiful, a gift if you ever hear it. This music is embodied here in

Rosslyn through the principles of sacred geometry. That is why you wanted to sing."

"And this music is healing. What does it do?"

"The music of the spheres is always healing and uplifting, Mary. Back in the days when St. Clair had Rosslyn built, people were not encouraged to sing. Oh, they had choirs but the laypeople in the church were not allowed to sing. The choirs did the singing."

Scratching her head, Mary looked hard at the gray stone chapel. "Okay, but there must be some specific reason St. Clair had the music of the spheres put into Rosslyn."

"Exactly," Nicholas said, pleased with her grasp of a huge overview of sacred geometry. "Music notes each have an energy expression of their own. When you place certain notes in combination with each other, something happens. It's a good thing, but it's magic in the moment. When these notes are played by instruments or sung by a human voice, we are able to connect directly to the Great Mother Goddess. After all, it is her music to begin with and she loves us. When that music is played or sung, we become part of a greater ceremony. It is a miracle."

"Have you heard her music?"

"Many times. To hear it is to be made whole

and of a peaceful nature. Her music takes away the heavy energy of the *Tupay,* which is why the *Tupay* are always trying to suppress what St. Clair knew when he built this chapel."

"Wow, and he did it under a Pope and confining religion. They were suppressing ancient cosmic truths that could benefit all of us."

He grinned. "Exactly." A robin flew down in front of them on the grassy lawn, intent on finding a worm. "I believe that music may be one of the keys to discovering those emerald spheres." He folded his hands in front of him, elbows resting on his thighs.

"It would make sense," Mary agreed, "but I'm no singer, Nicholas. And I don't play any musical instrument." Giving him a worried look, she added, "Does that mean the spheres won't appear?"

"I don't know," he admitted. "My sense of the situation is that the special and unique music encoded within Rosslyn has something to do with them. Why would the Incan man and woman who each carried a sphere bring them here? They must have been led here by spirits and then discovered the secret to this place."

"Hmm," Mary said. She enjoyed looking over at Nicholas. He was long, lanky and had a relaxed air about him. "The Emperor Pachacuti lived very early in the fifteenth century. Rosslyn had been completed by 1480. What I'd give to know what they discovered."

"I've tried to find that out in the Akashic Records," Nicholas said, "but that information has been removed to the Hall of Secrets."

"Hall of Secrets? What does that mean?"

"It means that some information is given out only to those who are ready for it and can understand it."

"So, we're on our own," she muttered.

"Yes, we are."

Mary shook her head. "I just don't know how the spheres will contact me. I'm worried now. I'm not some highly evolved being, I can't sing or play an instrument."

Sitting up, Nicholas reached out and laid his hand gently upon her slumped shoulder. "Don't be so glum," he urged. "Part of discovery is knowing and understanding. We'll walk around the chapel and each time we do, we will pick up more information."

Once more, his touch was electric. Mary felt his strong fingertips upon the fabric of her blouse. Her skin radiated with joyful little ripples of pleasure where his flesh connected with her. "I like your positive outlook," she said. "Besides, you can't see Rosslyn in just one walk-through. There're just too many layers to her."

Chapter 6

"My lord!" Lothar said as he rushed into Victor's office, "We've a lead on where the next emerald sphere is located!"

Victor Carancho Guerra looked up from his desk at his faithful knight, Lothar. Ordinarily, Victor would lash out at such disrespect for bursting into the office, but when Lothar mentioned the emerald sphere, he forgave him. "Indeed? Tell me more," he urged, indicating to the knight to shut the door so no one could overhear their conversation.

Lothar, a huge man with a round face and tiny

pig-like brown eyes, grinned widely. "My Lord, forgive my unexpected intrusion." He bowed toward Victor. "But one of our *Tupay* watchmen caught wind of something strange going on at Rosslyn Chapel, which sits near Edinburgh, Scotland." Waving his hands enthusiastically, Lothar continued, "He was having breakfast in the Original Roslin Inn near the chapel when two people came in. He saw the Vesica Pisces birthmarks on their necks. So, he keyed his hearing as he ate and listened. The woman is Mary Anderson, a quilt designer, and the other is a man named Nicholas. He heard them talking about an emerald sphere in the chapel itself!"

Victor grinned and rubbed his hands. "Well done, Lothar! This is exactly the break we needed."

Blushing at praise from the Dark Lord, Lothar pulled over a chair and sat down in front of the desk. "My lord, I would like to volunteer for this mission. Clearly, there is a sphere in the chapel. And I know you will want to follow these two Warriors for the Light. Obviously, they have been chosen by the sphere to find its exact location. All we have to do is hover nearby, wait and then grab it once it materializes somewhere in the chapel itself."

Victor pulled a bunch of information off his files behind him. These were energetic tablets and they had the ability to bring up anything Victor wanted. Laying his hand over one of the eight-by-ten tablets, he telepathed information on Rosslyn Chapel. When it emerged with text and photos, it flashed a red-light warning. That meant danger.

"Damn," Victor muttered, his black brows gathering at the root of his nose, "this isn't good."

Leaning forward, Lothar said, "What's wrong?"

Hearing the edge in his faithful knight's voice, Victor held up the tablet and handed it across the desk to him. "As you know, there are various places on Earth that are *Taqe* strongholds—places we cannot go or access. Rosslyn Chapel is one of them. It was built over the most powerful vortex in Scotland. The man who had it created was a Templar offspring through family lineage."

Groaning, Lothar rapidly read through the warning. "Templar? Of all things. They were Warriors for the Light, too." He grimaced and looked up at the Dark Lord. Victor wore a black goatee that made his narrow, very pale face even more powerful and sinister. The Dark Lord had been alive, ruling the Earth, for over four thousand years. Through Victor's efforts, males had kept females suppressed and subdued.

Since 1960, however, the *Taqe,* the People of the Light, had made serious inroads into this imbalance, and women were starting to assert their cosmic right to be equal to any male. That wasn't good for the *Tupay,* because the heavy energy was all about control and disempowering others. The Emerald Key Necklace, Lothar realized, was an attempt to bring women back into power on Earth. If that happened, the energy of the *Tupay* would be greatly reduced. And that could not be.

"That means," Lothar said, "that we aren't allowed into the chapel itself."

"Correct."

"But that doesn't mean we can't possess other human beings and hide behind their auras and demeanors and follow them."

"Usually that is correct," Victor said, leaning back and rocking in his black leather chair. He steepled his long, narrow fingers and looked up at the ceiling. "First, I want a background check on this Mary Anderson and on Nicholas. Find out all you can." He cursed softly. "I hate the fact we aren't allowed into the Akashic Records. It would make our job much easier if we could just go in there with the names and find out everything we needed."

"It's not fair," Lothar parroted. He brightened, stood and handed his Dark Lord the tablet. "However, I will set my office personnel on this task and get back to you as quickly as we can."

"Do that," Victor muttered.

Lothar returned to the office hours later. He brought with him two energy tablets with the information they'd researched on the two warriors.

Victor quickly read through them and his brows knitted. "Mary Anderson is the granddaughter of Jeff Anderson?" He looked across the desk to where Lothar sat.

"Yes, my lord, she is."

"That's not good," Victor said, stroking his goatee. "Does Jeff know about her being a Warrior for the Light?"

Opening his hands, he said, "I don't know, my lord. He is not *Taqe*. As you know, every spirit who wants to come here and work with us to support *Tupay* philosophy is thoroughly vetted to ensure that *Taqe* energy is not a part of their family genetics. I went over his entrance examination and Jeff Anderson is clean. He's *Tupay*."

"Then someone in his family after he died unknowingly married into a *Taqe* line of Warriors for the Light. Of all things…." Victor growled.

Lothar nodded. "I knew you would be unhappy about this development, my lord."

Victor sat back, thinking deeply. Jeff Anderson was an up-and-coming young spirit. He was a warrior by blood and energy. First, did he know or follow Mary Anderson and her life? If he did, he'd know sooner or later that she was directly involved in the hunt for the sphere. Further, Victor and his men on the missions had no problem possessing a *Taqe*. And if he needed to possess Mary Anderson, he'd do it in a heartbeat. Of course, when he dispossessed Mary, she'd die in five minutes, the silver cord to her spirit cut as he removed himself from within her body.

"This complicates things," Victor said, unhappy. "Jeff has proven himself a knight in the making for us. He's faithful and loyal. He proved himself on that mission he took with us a while back to try and steal the emerald sphere up in Banff, Canada."

"I know, my lord. I have been thinking about this dilemma, too."

"Well, it's not uncommon that *Tupay* intermarry with *Taqe* and vice versa. Jeff's line was *Tupay.* It's unfortunate one of his offspring married into *Taqe* after he died. But that's not his fault."

"How do you think he will react once he finds out his granddaughter is at the core of our mission?" Lothar asked with hesitation. "He knows we'll possess her if necessary. And she'll die afterward. I worry how he'll react."

Shrugging, Victor said, "He's taken the oath of the *Tupay*. He knows from his education here at the castle that families intermix between heavy and light energy. He shouldn't be surprised."

"But would he interfere with our mission to protect his granddaughter?" Lothar asked. "That's what we don't know, my lord."

Sitting up, Victor said, "He's proven himself already, Lothar. When the chips were down, Jeff did exactly as he was instructed. I think what is best here is to tell him nothing. We need to undertake this mission quietly. No one but your people and myself will know what's going on. The less said, the better. We'll leave Jeff here and he'll be none the wiser. I believe we can do this under the radar."

Worriedly, Lothar said, "I know we can keep our mission secret. But is he in psychic contact with his family? That is what we don't know. And if we send one of our trusted knights to invade his personal space to find out, he'll be outraged by the unexpected intrusion. That is akin to being energetically raped and we never do that to our knights in training. Jeff might never forgive you for that assault upon his person."

"I don't feel we need to do anything," Victor said, holding up his hand to cut off the conversation. "I'm sufficiently persuaded that Jeff Anderson isn't going to harm our mission. He's one of our finest young knights in training and frankly, people like him are too hard to come by. I don't want to sully the water with him if I don't have to, Lothar."

Bowing, Lothar murmured, "I understand, my lord. If Jeff wasn't at the top of his class and as psychically powerful as he is, it would be easy to imprison him in a cell here at the castle."

Victor nodded. "But we won't go that route." Sometimes in delicate cases like this, students were imprisoned for their own good while a mission went down. And, depending upon the student's reaction to being imprisoned for something done against their larger family on Earth, they might be destroyed by Victor himself, after the mission was accomplished. One thing Victor hated was a *Tupay* knight or soldier in training rebelling against him, but it was a rare occurrence. If it happened, Victor had to destroy the soul of the man.

Jeff Anderson was sleeping. He was restless, feeling as if something was very, very wrong. In a dream, he saw Mary Anderson, his granddaughter. The man named Nicholas was at her side. He could see their auras, each with silver in the outer rings, denoting they were Warriors for the Light. She was smiling. And then, Jeff saw the Dark Lord barreling in from the other dimension. He plunged into Mary's crown at the top of her head. He saw his granddaughter give a cry of distress and fall to her knees. Victor Carancho Guerra had possessed his beloved granddaughter!

Jeff shot up out of bed. He sobbed and his gasps came out in unsteady gulps. No! No, this could not be! It was dark outside. The *Tupay* stronghold had a twenty-four-hour time just as on Earth. He struggled to his feet, the coolness of the wood on his nightstand steadying him. Hand against his chest, the soft cotton of his pajama top damp with sweat, he paced. Was this a dream? A warning? Or had the Dark Lord already possessed Mary?

"God, no," he whispered unsteadily. "That can't have happened!"

Desperation wound around his stomach and he felt as if an invisible fist were squeezing it painfully hard. He hurried to the bathroom, poured himself some water and gulped it down. First things first. Jeff had had advanced training because he was in the apprentice knight program. He had to check on Mary.

Lying back down on his bed, the covers rumpled around him, he closed his eyes. He grounded himself and moved into an altered state. This gave him the ability to astral-travel anywhere he wanted and in any dimension. Willing his astral body to come out of the top of his head, the silver cord shining brightly between it and his body, Jeff pictured Mary's face.

In an instant, he was in a hotel room where she was sleeping. She was safe! She was turned on her right side, her hands tucked near her head, and he clearly saw the Vesica Pisces symbol on the back of her slender neck. His family, who had always been *Tupay,* had now started a new branch on their tree. His fingers tingled wildly. Jeff sensed that he was changing. He'd touched the green aura put out by the emerald sphere on the last mission, and it was affecting him.

As he hovered in a corner of Mary's room watching her sleep, Jeff felt the changes more powerfully. No longer did he want to support the *Tupay* way of living. He saw that heavy energy actually imprisoned a person's soul while the light energy freed a person. It didn't make living on Earth any easier, but it fed hope to the soul. Jeff was suddenly against war, assault and aggression as a way to control things, people and situations. He began to understand his granddaughter's love of peace, of wanting a peaceful Earth where all religions, skin colors and genders got along without strife, terror or murder.

Mary's aura had so many glittery pink and fuchsia colors in it, that it touched Jeff profoundly. Her aura was huge in comparison to those of other human beings. And the silver on the border of her outer fields was bright and beautiful. Jeff remained in her room, simply allowing the heart energy to saturate him. He found such a deep sense of love for his granddaughter, who was surely leading the Anderson clan toward a better way of living. She was freeing up the entire family with her light energy.

A sense of utter peace filled Jeff. He suddenly

"got" what the Warriors for the Light stood for. They wanted to remove the shackles of heavy energy and allow the Emerald Key Necklace's goodness to saturate the planet. It was a stunning realization for him, and his granddaughter would play an important role. Mary was courageous, chosen exactly for her purity.

As he remained in her room, Jeff began to realize that the dream had given him a warning. He had to protect Mary. A plan filtered into his consciousness and he was startled as a green-and-gold light encircled him.

Be at peace, my brother.

Jeff didn't know where the voice originated from. It was masculine, deep and not threatening. Mesmerized, he watched the green-and-gold light surround and embrace him. There was such a powerful sense of love moving through his aura that all he could do was sigh with relief. The light destroyed much of the darkness within him. Jeff felt as if he were part of an invisible world where only love, compassion and joy resided. He'd never felt like this before.

What are you? Who are you? he telepathed to the disembodied voice.

I am the spirit of the sixth emerald sphere. I am Faith. I am connecting with you because you have touched the energy that I contained before this. I am healing you, my brother. And when I am done, you must hear my plan. It will help to protect your granddaughter, who is one of us. Will you let me show you how to keep her safe?

Would he? Of course! *Yes, show me,* Jeff told the voice.

For the next two minutes, Jeff was given a visual of a plan. One that the sphere's spirit hoped would protect Mary Anderson. When it was done, Jeff felt shaken.

You want me to steal the emerald sphere from the hands of the Dark Lord? That seemed impossible! If he were caught, he'd instantly be killed. And then he could not protect Mary at all.

My brother, it must be attempted. By absconding with the emerald, the Dark Lord's attention might be pulled away from your granddaughter. Then, as he searches for the stolen sphere, Mary and Nicholas can find us and take us home to the Village of the Clouds.

Jeff felt shell-shocked. The green-and-gold energy continued to nurture him like a mother holding her beloved infant. *But I don't have that kind of skill. The emerald sphere is in the Dark Lord's office and in an energy safe. How can I get to it?* he asked.

We will help you. I have infused your heart with the Taqe *energy. I have left everything else about you alone. To the* Tupay, *you appear to be* Tupay. *But inwardly, you are now a Warrior for the Light. No one will know or be able to know of your change. You will not wear the Vesica Pisces birthmark. When you go to his office, I will work with you and work through you to retrieve my stolen spiritual sister.*

While he nodded his assent, Jeff felt fear and anxiety encircle his gut. *You can do this?* he demanded, unsure. How could love undo an energy safe? Jeff did not know.

We are sure. Remember—this is being done to try and protect your granddaughter while she comes to find us. She must do certain things before we can appear to her. And that is between her and us. We can work with you to retrieve the stolen emerald sphere.

And if I do retrieve it, what then? Jeff asked. *What do I do with it? Where do I go? I am not allowed in the Village of the Clouds because I'm* Tupay.

Be at ease, my brother. The elders from the village already know what has happened to you and that you are changing sides to join us. Once you get the sphere in your hands, we will take

*you to them. At the foot of the bridge, Alaria will
meet and greet you. You must understand that
once you cross that bridge back to the Village of
the Clouds, you can never go back to the* Tupay
castle. You will be one of us.

Confused, Jeff considered the information.
He'd never been a turncoat. He'd been an army
Ranger. He was patriotic, a man of his word. Jeff
prided himself on his loyalty. *Will the Dark Lord
know the sphere has been stolen?*

*Yes, immediately. We hope by doing this, it
will give our human team a chance to find us
without interference from the* Tupay. *It is a
chance, but nothing is ever guaranteed until it
happens. As you know, a human's will and ability to change their reality is the most powerful
skill they have on Earth. We can create this
opening, this possibility. We hope the Dark
Lord will go back to his castle to search for the
lost emerald sphere, but that is not assured.
Free-will choice is available to all, regardless
of the dimension they live within. All we can do
is create a strategy and hope they will fall for
the trap.*

Jeff watched Mary sleeping like an angel. His
heart tugged mightily with love for his granddaughter. She carried his tainted blood. Yet, she

had a higher calling, and it was to the betterment of the Earth and all its citizens. As he digested the information, his gaze never leaving his granddaughter, Jeff made up his mind. *All right, I'll do it. I've never been a traitor. I feel like one. But I love my granddaughter more than my life.*

My brother, you truly are a Warrior for the Light. They have the highest calling and are willing to sacrifice their lives for the good of all. And what are you betraying? A way of life in heavy energy which you now know simply imprisons souls and stops them from spiritual advancement that is rightfully theirs. You are not a traitor, Jeff Anderson. You have great courage and you have put your love of your granddaughter above the calling of becoming a Tupay *knight. Surely, you are worthy in the eyes of the* Taqe. *We ask the blessing of the Great Mother Goddess upon you.*

Jeff shook his head. *Don't bother. Right now I'm scared to death. I don't want to die, but even more important, I don't want Mary possessed. She'll die.*

We cannot promise her life will be spared, but we are trying to protect her. Nicholas de Beaufort is a French Cathar monk and Templar knight. He has been trained in the energy warfare arts and will be Mary's main protection. He will give his life for hers if it is necessary.

As will I, Jeff said grimly. No way was a member of his family going to be targeted and used by the Dark Lord like this.

Chapter 7

The August afternoon was warm and Mary needed some time alone. Nicholas seem to sense this and left. He got a reservation for her at the Original Roslin Inn and then went to buy some more clothes. She'd told him she wanted to get used to the energy of the chapel grounds. He'd agreed with her strategy.

As Mary sat on one of the wooden benches on the west side of the chapel, her gaze moved across the well-manicured lawn. Hundreds of tourists from around the world meandered around the beautiful chapel. The trees were well-placed as were graves from Sinclairs who had passed on. Pruned bushes and flowers surrounded each rectangular gravestone marker. Mary swore she could almost smell the ocean, which wasn't that far away. Moving her shoulders, the sunlight dappling down across her from where the bench stood beneath an old chestnut tree, she smiled and closed her eyes.

The sense of peace surrounding Rosslyn Chapel was palpable. She'd noticed earlier how many of the tourists seemed exceedingly relaxed within the confines of the property.

From her own travels, Mary had learned that the energy of sacred places fed a person's spirit and heart. That was why she loved going to ancient sites and temples; they made her even more fervent about living in her heart on a daily basis.

Indigenous peoples around the world also knew where there were major lines of energy known as ley lines, as well as vortexes. Mary could tell that a vortex whirled powerfully where the chapel had been built. It was then that she became aware of another presence.

Feeling no threat, Mary remained in her altered state, eyes closed and her clairvoyant ability ready to see into the other dimensions. In front of her was a ghost. Or, more aptly, a spirit of a woman dressed in a long white gown. A hood fell across her black hair. Her large, luminous blue eyes shone with such light that Mary was transfixed.

Peace, my sister, Mary signaled, using telepathy. In her experience such places of power always had a guardian. Was this woman Rosslyn's guardian? Mary absorbed the nurturing energy that emanated from the woman who watched her.

Peace be to you, my sister. I am Sophia, guardian of this sacred place.

I am Mary. Welcome. Have I offended you, Sophia? Mary knew that in many sacred places, gifts had to be brought, usually ones from nature like cornmeal, grain, flowers or food. And asking for permission to enter was also accepted ceremonial protocol. Had she made a mistake, and was the guardian coming to correct the situation?

Holding up her hand, which had been hidden within the long sleeves of her white robe, Sophia smiled. *You could never offend me. I came to welcome you.*

Thank you, my sister. Mary felt the incredible power around Sophia. She was much more than a guardian, and yet, she cloaked her power so that Mary couldn't sense more of who she really was.

You have come for the two emerald spheres.

Mary's heart took off at a fast beat. *I have.*

You received a dream from them. They called you here.

Mary nodded. *That is so, Sophia.* A smile lingered on the mature woman's lips. Her eyes glinted with amusement. Mary felt as if this woman guardian was a very old, old soul.

You must know that the Dark Lord of the Tupay *wants these two emerald spheres. Are you aware of that?*

My protector, Nicholas, said he would find us sooner or later, Mary answered.

He will kill you for those spheres.

A cold shiver moved down Mary's spine. The sun was warm on her shoulders, the wind soft and filled with the scent of fresh-cut grass, but it didn't minimize the terror within her. Seeing the seriousness in Sophia's broad, beautiful face, the black curls peeking out around the edges of her hood, Mary grimaced. *That scares me.*

It should. The Dark Lord already has one sphere. He will want these last two, Sophia warned.

Where do you stand on this? Mary asked. Guardians, in her experience, fluctuated on their loyalties. They were given a set of strict orders and never deviated from them. Was Sophia friend or foe? Was she pro-*Tupay?* Or was she of the Light? Not all guardians here on Earth were *Taqe.*

Opening her long-fingered hands, Sophia gestured around the chapel. *I want you to see the energy surrounding the chapel....*

Suddenly, Mary saw what she hadn't seen before, a bubble of white-and-gold light surrounding the chapel. In some ways it reminded Mary of a huge soap bubble with gorgeous rainbow colors rippling across the dome. *This is the protection for the chapel?* she queried Sophia.

It is. Part of it, Sophia amended. *What you need to see and know is here.*

Taking a deep breath, Mary hoped she didn't offend the guardian. *Are you* Taqe? Tupay?

Laughing, Sophia opened her arms and said, *I am all that is, ever has been or ever will be.*

When Sophia laughed, the energy around her aura glowed with such life and bright intensity that Mary was nearly blinded. Without thinking, she held up her hand against her closed eyes. Later, she would realize it was a dumb thing to do because the brightness had nothing to do with her human eyes; it had to do with her third eye that gave her sight into the other dimensions. As Sophia's laughter ended, the glow also ebbed. In its place Mary saw Sophia's aura once more. Who was this woman?

Tell me, Sophia, are you here at Rosslyn Chapel for a special reason? Is this chapel important to all people on this Earth?

Sophia eyed her with a glint of amusement. *My child, Rosslyn is the seventh center of power here on this side of Mother Earth. There is a sacred spiritual path that begins in what you call Europe. Six of the centers are located there. The seventh and most important one for the pilgrim who goes to each is here at Rosslyn.*

Mary recalled Nicholas telling her about the other six Gothic churches in Europe that were stepping stones for spiritual evolvement. *Yes, I'm familiar with them.*

Sophia once more wrapped her hands within the folds of her long, wide sleeves. *Few know of these seven sacred centers. Yet, on each continent there is a set of seven chakras. They are there to promote health for Mother Earth. Long ago your kind found them. They honored them in ceremony, with song and voice. Over time humans built rock circles, then temples and now these churches rest upon these powerful sites. But each time there were people who knew and understood what they were really about. Are you familiar with chakras?*

Mary inclined her head. *Each human has nine of them. The chakras begin at the tailbone and go up through the abdomen, the solar plexus, the heart, throat, brow and the final and seventh one is located in the top of our head. Are those the chakras you are speaking about?* Mary wanted to make sure.

Yes, we are talking of the same thing, Sophia said. She turned and gestured toward Rosslyn. *Rosslyn represents the crown chakra on the journey across Europe. Anyone who walks into each of these secret places in the correct order, will experience a oneness with the Great Mother Goddess. They will be healed, uplifted and come to understand what the wisdom of the heart already knows.*

Mary smiled. *I don't know of anyone who wouldn't want to evolve and be a part of the love that always surrounds us.* All the ancient texts spoke of this but the key was tuning into this ever-present love energy. For some, it was known as the Philosopher's Stone or the ability to turn lead into gold. This process had been spoken about in many different ways and terms and yet, Mary understood from Sophia that there was a shortcut available to humans, which was good news. One didn't have to become an alchemist or study the ancient mysteries. All one had to do was have faith and believe and move sincerely through all of these churches to accomplish the same thing. Another road to Rome, so to speak.

Indeed, Sophia said, turning back and facing Mary. *Perhaps you do not know this, but long ago, you took this initiation. You had a lifetime as a young woman who traveled by foot and survived the long, arduous journey because you were a midwife. You were able to stop at each area for a year and devote yourself to the people of that region as well as to the energy of that sacred chakra.*

Amazed, Mary stared at Sophia. *I did?*

Laughing, Sophia shook her head. *Do you not wonder why you were chosen to come here? It is one thing to hold one emerald sphere. To hold two of them? Well, you must have a powerful spiritual background and be completely heart-centered.*

Mary smiled a little. *I don't feel that powerful or gifted, Sophia. I love designing and teaching women how to make beautiful quilts.*

Ah, yes, but do you ever wonder why you have reached the pinnacle within that craft? Why you are famous around the world? And why your designs sell so well?

Mary frowned. *No, I hadn't really looked at myself in that way. I love drawing the designs and women seem to love them as much as I do.*

That is because your designs are ancient, forgotten symbols, but you are bringing them back once more to this age and time. Your designs are archetypal and that means when you create such designs, you automatically tap into their energy. And archetypal energy always lifts and heals. And that is what you do, my child.

That's wonderful to know, Mary said.

Some people are messengers. Some write, some draw, some sing, some play an instrument. You create quilt designs. Little do the people know when they sleep beneath one of your archetypal designs, that it is healing them. That is a wonderful gift and that is why your work is famous.

Mary smiled fully. *Thank you for all of that. I never thought of myself in those ways. I just aspire to make people happy.*

Which is why you are here with me. I watched you today as you moved through Rosslyn. You felt at home here, did you not?

Absolutely. I was enthralled with the stone

sculptures, but it was the energy, particularly coming from the crypt area, that drew me.

The crypt area is at the center of the vortex, which is why you were drawn to it. Long ago, the crypt housed a ceremonial stone circle of great power. The chapel above it came much later. Although everyone is drawn to the chapel, the real power resides in the crypt. Intuitively, you know that you need to read the symbols on the walls to discover the order with which to trigger a cascade of energy events. This will allow the emerald spheres to reveal themselves in the third dimension.

Oh. Mary stared at all-knowing Sophia. *Is there something I should do or say?* Sacred ceremony often meant speaking certain words or phrases. It could involve singing a song or playing an instrument. Was there some movement that she needed to repeat in order to trip this energy sequence? Each sacred site had keys to opening its doors. And each was different, which was why working with the guardian was vital.

Sophia stared into Mary's eyes. *In order to be worthy of receiving these spheres you must make love to Nicholas de Beaufort.*

Stunned, Mary stared open-mouthed at the guardian. *What?*

The world has been scourged of women being in their rightful place to men. For the last five thousand years, men have ruled with male-dominated religion in order to subjugate women and control them. Sophia's voice shook with sadness. *And it has left this world in shambles. Men without women as equal partners cannot change what will happen here in 2012.*

The dire threat overwhelmed her shock over the directive to make love with Nicholas. *I agree that women are not considered equals to men. But that is changing slowly.*

Too slowly, Sophia pronounced, frowning.

Mary felt the sadness deep within Sophia and she heard it in her lowered tone. *What then? Are we headed for the abyss? Is there no turning this crisis around?*

Yes, and it involves you and Nicholas. Each of you is a stellar example of an evolved human being. You both work from your heart. You live and practice compassion. There is great love for this Earth and all who live upon it. Essentially, you are equal in all ways. One is man and the other is woman. You are the perfect mates for one another.

But I don't understand why I have to make love to Nicholas. I barely know him and he's my guardian, not my lover. Mary began to feel anxious. It was one thing to be drawn to Nicholas and quite another being ordered to go to bed with him.

Sophia held up her hands. *Before you say anything more, I will show you several of your incarnations with one another. As you may know, we incarnate with a group of similar souls who want to evolve at a certain rate. Watch...*

The world tilted, and Mary sensed she was no longer sitting on the bench. The warmth from the sunlight disappeared. There was rushed movement, a feeling that she was rotating in a large, unseen circle. Where was she being taken? Mary tried to choke back her fear. Sophia had been kind and loving, not threatening. But Mary had run into dangerous sorcerers from time to time who posed as guardians. Despite this, Mary felt as if Sophia was her ally, not her enemy.

The movement halted. The world dissolved into colors in front of her closed eyes. A thick leather-bound book decorated with filigreed gold in the form of a double circle appeared. Her name was written in gold on it. As Sophia stood to her left, Mary asked, *Where are we?*

The Hall of the Akashic Records, Sophia said. She pointed to the book. It was closed with a thick gold clasp. *Open it. This is a record of all your lifetimes….*

Mary felt excitement and curiosity as she unsnapped the clasp. With both hands, she opened the book. As she did, she saw in the contents contained through thousands of lifetimes. Amazed, she leaned over to see dates of birth, of death, where she had been, what genders she had been and her names. *This…is me?* she asked, slowly turning each thick parchment-like page. *These are all my lifetimes so far?* There were thousands!

Sophia smiled. *Your entire book looks like this. In order to view a lifetime, you need only press your finger on one of the written lines. Then, look up.* She pointed in front of them. The mist that surrounded them began to dissolve.

Mary saw a monitor like an enormous television screen, and her heart pounded with anticipation. She had heard of the Akashic records. But never had she remembered being in this famous hall. She recalled seeing this book in her dreams, but never opening it. Looking over at the guardian, she asked, *Is there a certain lifetime I should view?*

Sophia pointed to one of them. *Choose this one, my child.*

Chapter 8

After visiting the Hall of the Akashic Records and coming out of her altered state, Mary sat shaken. The sun had shifted. Her eyes focused and changed. Her vision sharpened and became clear once more. The warmth had moved from the top of her head to her left side.

How long had she been gone? Looking at her watch, she noted an hour had passed. Mary grounded herself in the third dimension, which she called home. The gray stone walls of Rosslyn Chapel rose before her, gleaming in the afternoon sunlight. Birds were singing melodically across the lawn.

As she flexed her hands in her lap, her mind spun with the new information on her incarnations. Over and over, she had had lifetimes with Nicholas de Beaufort. The love between them was as solid as a rock. Sophia had explained that they were soul mates in the truest sense of the words. That was why she felt nearly obsessive about being in his arms, wanting to kiss him and love him. Those lifetimes, hundreds of them, explained everything for Mary about her reaction to the French knight-monk.

Even more surprising, in spirit she had chosen the path to be a priestess. In today's world, she would be called a pagan. Back in those many lifetimes, she was a priestess or a priest tied to Mother Earth as a healer and servant to the people of her village. So many times, she was the ceremonial person representing the village to the living spirits that surrounded them. That explained why she was so incredibly psychic in her current lifetime. Sophia had told her that any mystical skills she brought were earned from past lifetimes and could be used now.

Her heart beat in her breast like a wild bird wanting to be released. Touching her chest, her fingertips resting against the material of her T-shirt, Mary sighed. Oh, how she loved

Nicholas! She saw him taking the warrior's route in his many lifetimes. He knew how to fight, to defend and build a powerful amount of energy in this particular soul path. Her energy was equal to his, but created from a different place. Their powers overlapped, forming the perfect union.

They were the ideal bookends. One was a warrior, the other a sage. The only problem, Sophia had told her, was that Nicholas had been so traumatized by being burned alive at the stake, he'd refused further physical incarnations. While it was the choice of his soul to decide that, it had stopped him from continuing to develop spiritually in his heart. With Mary coming to him as a woman, she could open his heart and allow his anger and hopelessness to dissolve. That would make him her equal in every way. Until then, the load and responsibility fell on Mary's shoulders because her heart was clear and steady.

Taking a deep breath, Mary realized this mission was in fragile balance. The outcome was not assured at all. What if Nicholas did not want her? Would he refuse to make love to her? Mary rubbed her brow, feeling a mild headache coming on. Her poor aura had been beaten up in this process.

What to do? Nicholas was probably back at the hotel. Should she go to his room and tell him everything? Or just come to him and see if he'd accept her? Mary found that the easy part. There was such a fullness of love in her heart for this gallant, knightly man, that she hungered to mate with him, be one with him. He was so wounded by his last lifetime. She ached to heal that part of Nicholas, to free him from that dark, dark cage that kept his soul a prisoner.

Standing, Mary smoothed down the fabric of her skirt. The sun was warm and nurturing, like Sophia. Many people were now visiting Rosslyn, the busses stopping with great frequency and unloading those who were drawn to this magical and healing place. She now had to take an important step to bring about Nicholas's healing.

Nicholas had just put his new clothes into the dresser drawers when there was a knock at his door. He'd closed down a lot of his sensory ability while in Edinburgh. Any city was a place of noise pollution, which hindered his senses. He wasn't sure who could be at his door but he knew enough that it was no threat. As he opened the door, he saw Mary and happiness thrummed through him.

"Hi, Nicholas. How was your shopping trip?" Mary stood uncertainly. Even though she now knew a lot about them as a couple, she was still in human form with a particular personality. She didn't see herself playing the vamp and seducing Nicholas. Her hands were clasped in front of her, and she hoped he didn't see her confusion.

"Come in." He greeted her with a welcoming smile and stepped aside. Her hair was softly windblown. He couldn't help but yearn for her. There was nothing but beauty about Mary and he itched to touch her, explore her and drag her into his arms. All of those desires shocked him because of his monkish attitudes toward women and a physical life. Now, he wished he could break away from that. He wanted Mary in every way.

"Thanks." Mary moved into his large, well-appointed room, which was filled with dark wooden antiques evoking the Victorian era. Her body tingled from head to toe as she watched him shut the door. He was dressed in a red polo shirt, dark brown tweed trousers and dark brown leather shoes. The red material was stretched across his massive chest, his shoulders automatically thrown back with pride. "Hey, you look very Scottish. I like your new look."

Feeling heat come to his face, Nicholas looked down at his new clothes. "They feel awkward. The shoes…" He pointed at them. "I'd rather be wearing a good pair of boots."

Laughing softly, Mary moved around the room. Her heart was beating hard. She touched the dresser with her fingertips and went over to the window with its lacy white curtains running across. "Shades of being a Templar knight?" she wondered, meeting his narrowing eyes. Her breath hitched. Nicholas wanted her. There it was: raw and feral. Excitement bubbled up through her. Before, she'd not been certain of his attraction to her, but now she was. Joy skittered through her and she felt an ache beginning between her legs. Oh, just to love this precious man. He was so solicitous, sensitive and caring. And yet, as Mary met and held his gaze, she felt his heart wound. It was a wound that kept him imprisoned in the past and unable to move forward spiritually.

Giving her an embarrassed chuckle, Nicholas said, "I suppose so."

"What else did you buy?" Mary looked at the opened closet and then at his mahogany dresser.

"I like the polo shirts." He touched his chest. "They remind me of wearing chain mail beneath my tunic."

"That's good," Mary deadpanned, an inescapable grin tugging at the corners of her mouth. "But, no helmet this time, right?"

Her teasing lifted the darkness that surrounded his heart. "No helmet and no shield." She was light and playful. And he couldn't get enough of looking into her sparkling blue eyes. The smile on her full mouth sent a shock of heat down through him. For a moment, Nicholas felt his breath stolen from his body, such was the power she had over him. Nicholas was sorry he hadn't gotten to the Hall of Akashic Records to look up Mary and understand their incarnations together. He was very sure they'd been together many times in the past.

Mary saw the stormy desire in his green eyes. Nicholas was a hunter. Feral. A predator of the top order. More like an eagle who had sighted his quarry than the man standing relaxed before her. "Good thing swords aren't in vogue right now," she managed, a little breathless over his expression. How utterly handsome he was! There was a rugged quality to him and the scar on his cheek made him even more desirable. His face showed that he was mature, thoughtful and in charge of himself on all levels. But was he attracted to her enough?

"Yes," he said, automatically touching his left hip where his sword had hung at one time, "they aren't welcome in this period on Earth."

Gulping, Mary decided to come clean. She remained near the window and wanted that distance between them. Being too close to Nicholas threatened her control over her desire for him. All she wanted to do now was wrap her arms around his thick, strong neck, stand on tiptoe and kiss his mouth. Mary knew she could heal him. That was a woman's gift to any man. "Nicholas, I need to sit down and share something that happened to me just now. Do you have the time?"

"Of course," he said, some of his desire tamped down by the serious look in her eyes. He pulled out one of the Victorian-era chairs and offered it to her. "Sit down." And then he walked over to the desk and pulled out a second chair. Nicholas was mindful to keep a reasonable distance between them. That was his nature, to be aware and respectful of women. "Now, what happened out there?"

"And that's the whole experience, Nicholas." Gulping, Mary clung to his darkened gaze. Nicholas was frowning, his hands on his long thighs, his mouth drawn in at the corners. She felt wave after wave of confusing feelings. "I felt it best to share it with you."

Dragging in a deep breath, he stared at her for a long moment. "Sophia…" he murmured. "I didn't realize she was the guardian here at Rosslyn. We haven't been here long enough to really begin exploring all the energies that are a part of this chapel and surrounding area."

"I know," Mary said. Buffeted by his raw feelings, Mary placed a protective bubble around her so it would absorb most of the energy and leave her more centered and less distracted. She worried what Nicholas thought about making love to her. She couldn't read him clearly because he was very upset over her experience with Sophia at the Hall of the Akashic Records. It killed her to sit still and remain quiet. Was he repelled by the possibility? He seemed to know more about Sophia than she did. Was the look on his face disgust? She curled her hands in her lap, unsure.

Nicholas got to his feet and began to pace the length of the room on the other side of the bed. His hands were behind his back, his head bent, gaze on the floor. Inwardly, he soared and crashed emotionally. Sophia wanted him to make love to Mary. Oh, sweet God, how he wanted to do just that! But his oath to Madeline, his wife of that lifetime, forbade such an alliance with another woman. And yet, Sophia had given the order. What should he do? Running his long fingers through his hair, Nicholas was consumed with indecision and anxiety. Because he had chosen to keep the personality of his last incarnation in spirit, he had this stumbling block. If he'd released that personality, he'd have no problem in making love with Mary. To do that, he'd have to release that lifetime, and he wasn't sure he could do that. Literally, Nicholas was caught betwixt and between by his own soul's choice.

"Do you know who Sophia is?" he asked suddenly, halting and pinning Mary with a sharpened look.

"Uh…no. You do, though. Who is she?"

"She *is* the Great Mother Goddess, Mary. She takes on the guise of Sophia, who was always known as a wise woman goddess here on Earth far back beyond the time of the Sumerian people of the Middle East. She is known by many names—Ishtar, Isis and Mary Magdalene, among others."

Mary's fingers flew to her lips. "Oh…dear… that's why she felt so powerful to me!"

Giving her a wry look, Nicholas drawled, "I dare say, Mary, she was heavily cloaked to stop her energy from completely destroying you. No one can look upon the Great Mother Goddess with their eyes for they will instantly die. Her auric vibration is so high and powerful that it would turn us to instant dust." He snapped his fingers. "If she truly unveiled herself completely to a mere human being, that is."

Mary gasped. "This is as if a religious person down here met the male God."

"The same thing," Nicholas said, heaviness in his tone. He paced again for several moments, and then halted and turned on his heel. "Sophia's request is, well, torturing me, Mary."

She heard the swell of emotion in his deep voice and saw the tortured look he gave her. "What do you mean? I don't understand." Did he not want to love her?

Opening his hands, he said bleakly, "I am stuck in the fourteenth century, Mary. I have the same traits, beliefs and personality as I did as a Templar knight." He gave her an anguished look. "I gave a vow to Sophia, whom we worshipped within the Templars, to remain true and loyal to my wife, Madeline." Lifting his head, he sucked in a ragged breath. And then, the words low and torn, he whispered, "I cannot make love with you, Mary. I would be breaking my vow. If I did that, I wouldn't really be a Templar knight or a Cathar monk. My kind was pure of heart and deed, both the men and women who served Sophia. We believed in a Great Mother Goddess." Grimacing, he added, "And that was our great secret that was never told to the world."

Mary felt a heavy weight descend upon her shoulders. Frowning, she engaged Nicholas's gaze. "If you were to keep this vow, Nicholas, why on earth would Sophia asked you to break it now? I don't understand."

Sitting down, he placed his elbows on his thighs with hands clasped in front of him. "Sophia knows my vow is an allegiance to my last incarnation. After I was burned to death, the Inquisition tortured Madeline and they murdered her. Sophia knows I cannot break this vow so long as I choose to retain the personality from that incarnation."

Mary didn't understand the complexity of incarnations and lifetimes as he was presenting it. "You're no longer in the fourteenth century, Nicholas. This is the twenty-first century. You did keep your vow to Madeline."

"Yes and no," he said.

Mary began to understand his angst. Sophia

had warned her that because Nicholas refused to have future lifetimes, the shock and trauma of his death superseded everything else. He was afraid to feel the pain of that incarnation and that was the reason he maintained the personality from that time. Who wasn't afraid of pain? Mary felt nothing but compassion toward Nicholas.

How she wanted to leap out of the chair, throw her arms around him and drag him into that bed, only a few feet away. Mary understood that if she tried to do that, more harm than good would result. Healing would not take place because Nicholas had not wrestled his way through reliving the pain from so long ago.

"The only person who can give you permission to dissolve that lifetime is you, Nicholas," she told him quietly. "I can't force you to relive that burning death. Nor can Sophia, for all her power and authority."

Shaking his head, Nicholas muttered, "Sophia never interferes in the lives of humans. She allows us to make and live with our own choices. We are responsible for what we choose. And she wouldn't force me to relive that incarnation unless I agreed to do it." Terror rippled through

Nicholas. Could he stand those feelings, the panic, the pain once again?

Mary remained silent and saw the anguish in Nicholas's face. He hid nothing from her. And she so desperately wanted to protect, heal and love him. Words leaped from her lips. "Do you want to love me, Nicholas?" Mary knew she shouldn't ask, but she couldn't help it. She felt as if she would die if she didn't know his answer.

His head snapped up. His eyes narrowed. Nicholas gave her a fierce look. "Of course I want to make love to you, Mary. From the first moment I saw you, I wanted you. Now I understand why. We are soul mates. There is a deep, indescribable yearning that occurs when soul mates meet in a common lifetime." He sat up and rubbed his sweaty palms against his thighs. "Want you? Woman, I want to breathe you into my heart, my soul. I never want to let you go. All I can think about, dream about, is loving you until you swoon with ecstasy within my arms." And all that stood in the way was to suffer once again. Could he do it?

Giving a small gasp, Mary felt desperate to embrace Nicholas. The look in his eyes was a mixture of grief, desire and frustration. He wanted her. But she had to maintain a grip on herself and let him act by his own conscience.

"And I want you," she managed in a quavering voice. "Nicholas, when I saw you, I felt my heart rip out of me. All I wanted to do was hand you my heart. I knew inside that you would be tender and gentle with me. I knew that in my soul. When Sophia allowed me to see certain lifetimes with you, I understood this wild, unfettered and unreasoning yearning I had the first time I laid eyes on you."

He held her tearful gaze. Mary was fighting valiantly not to cry, her eyes huge and luminous, her soft mouth parted with such a tragic expression, lips he wanted to kiss. Lips he wanted to feather and tease until she cried out in joy over his ability to make sweet, wild love with her. Shaking his head, his voice raw and low, he said, "I don't know what to do, Mary. I truly don't."

Nodding, Mary struggled to contain her emotional response, her love for Nicholas. Look, but don't touch. Dream, but no reality. More tears squeezed into her eyes. "Maybe we need to focus on the spheres, then," she suggested, clearing her throat. Forcing the tears away, Mary knew she had to move Nicholas gently from his inner turmoil to why they had met in the first place.

Heaving to his feet, Nicholas stared past her and out the window that looked out upon Rosslyn Chapel. "Yes, you're a wise woman, but then you always have been." Looking down at her, his eyes softened and he felt overwhelming love for this small woman with curly black hair and luminous blue eyes. "You've always been wise. This is the course we must follow. There is great danger to us. And we mustn't be distracted by our predicament with one another. If we don't focus, we can be killed, Mary." He stared at her hard for a long moment. "And I will not allow the Dark Lord to harm you in any way. That is my vow."

A chill worked its way up Mary's spine. For a moment, time halted and she swore she saw Nicholas once again as a mighty Templar knight in full costume. Instead of Scottish modern clothes, he wore chain mail beneath a white tunic that fell to below his knees with a bright red cross splashed across the chest. He was girded with two sword belts and beneath his left arm was his silver helmet with an eye slit. How handsome he was!

She knew she had not been in that lifetime with him. Soul mates didn't always incarnate together. When they did, it was a blessing—or a curse.

Moistening her lips, she saw the transparency dissolve and his presence in the now. "We're in this together, Nicholas. My life is no more or less important than yours. We were chosen to do this together. We're a good team, you and I." And she managed a small smile, her heart racing with so much love that it hurt to breathe.

Standing, Nicholas nodded. "Somehow, we must be a team, love one another from a distance and find those spheres."

Mary wondered what Nicholas would do with Sophia's decree that they must love one another. Judging by the turmoil in Nicholas's eyes, he was wrestling with that order, too. It wasn't up to her to demand anything of this courageous Templar knight. It was his decision to make and she would abide by whatever he chose to do. Like Sophia, she would not manipulate, change or push another person into the choice she wanted them to make. No, in the spiral of Life, everyone had their choices to make—on their own. But how was she going to quell her love for her soul mate? How?

Chapter 9

"We have to move now," Victor Guerra told the two men in his office. Both were knights for the *Tupay*. One was Lothar, who had accompanied him on his last mission to Banff National Park in Alberta, Canada. The other was a grizzled Roman centurion by the name of Marcus. In his last life, he'd served under Julius Caesar for nearly twenty years. Victor wanted a certified warrior with him on this trip as they left their fourth-dimension castle in the center of the *Tupay* empire.

Lothar nodded. "We'll possess three people and go undercover as usual? That way our auras will be hidden from this Mary Anderson and her guard dog, that Templar knight, Nicholas de Beaufort."

"Exactly," Victor said, rising from behind his desk. His office had huge heads of animals hung on the walls along with various weapons he had used in his earthly incarnations. Those days were long gone, but Victor liked the weapons he'd used. "We need to remain invisible to everyone and watch them for a while. Rosslyn Chapel it is off-limits to *Tupay*."

"Besides," Lothar added, wanting to please the Dark Lord, "I found out that the White Lady of the Chapel is none other than Sophia, the Great Mother Goddess, in disguise. That tells me how important this place is to the *Taqe*."

Stroking his pointed black-and-gray goatee, Victor nodded. "She often takes disguises on several important and sacred sites to the *Taqe* around the Earth." Victor saw Marcus frown. His face was square and he was built like a pit bull. The scars on his face, the broken nose, all conspired to make him look dangerous and sinister. Indeed, his dark brown eyes glittered with feral interest when he heard them speak.

"My lord," Marcus growled, "if this is so, how can we operate with the Mother there? Do you think she'll expand her circle of protection around them, too?"

It was a good question. Victor shrugged. "No. The Mother will not interfere in the fate of humans. So long as we don't make the mistake of entering the bubble of white light around the chapel itself, she'll remove herself from whatever else goes on."

Marcus wasn't satisfied. He stood in a red tunic that hung to his knees, a leather breastplate over his powerful upper body and a short sword at his side. Beneath his left arm was his leather helmet with a red horse-tail crest upon it. "And you know this for a fact?"

"I do," Victor said with authority. "I have operated with impunity around other power sites that were sacred to the *Taqe* and which she protected, and she did not interfere. Stop worrying, Marcus. I want your focus on Nicholas de Beaufort. He is a warrior's warrior. I'm sure you've done your homework on who and what he is?"

Bowing, Marcus said, "Of course I have, my lord. It is my duty to take him on when you rush in to steal the next emerald sphere after Mary Anderson retrieves it from the chapel." His small brown eyes grew savage and he patted the short sword on his left hip. "Not to worry, my lord. De Beaufort is mine. I've killed over a thousand men with my short sword. He will be just another one of them who has fallen beneath its fine, sharpened blade."

Victor nodded. Privately, he knew Marcus was considered the best warrior the *Tupay* had. Usually, he trained *Tupay* knights in the art of warfare at the academy. Marcus had spent his last lifetime as the centurion in Caesar's army, cut down by a blue-skinned Britain who had killed him during a battle. Marcus had come directly to the *Tupay* castle to work in spirit. He'd been a good teacher and was well respected. Victor felt good that Marcus was with them on this mission because he knew de Beaufort was utterly dangerous. The Templar would take no prisoners, his passion funneled into guarding Mary Anderson with the last breath he took. Victor hoped that Marcus would get the opportunity to slay the Templar. Once he was out of the way physically speaking, he would not be dangerous in spirit. Then Mary Anderson would be open and ready to be plundered once she obtained the sphere. Victor knew she was harmless and that suited his plans.

"Now what?" Lothar asked, eager to get the mission underway.

"Not so fast," Victor said. "Where is Jeff Anderson?"

"He's at the academy in his class," Lothar said.

"And he appears not to know that we're leaving to focus on his granddaughter?"

Shrugging, Lothar said, "My lord, his aura looks fine. I pick up no worry or knowledge that his granddaughter was chosen to retrieve the next emerald sphere."

Rubbing his hands together, Victor said, "Excellent." Turning, he opened the wall safe behind his desk. In there was one emerald sphere. He removed the energy web around the door and opened it. The sphere glowed a subdued green with flashes of gold within it. Satisfied, Victor closed the safe door and once more placed a web of energy around it. That way, if someone tried to tamper with it, he'd be instantly alerted and would blink back into the castle to catch and kill the culprit.

"All right," he murmured, "we're ready. When we go to Rosslyn Chapel, we'll hang around and observe. I'll choose three people to possess and take over their bodies. We need to find people who live in the area so that it's not some tourist."

Lothar grinned. "I'm ready, my lord!"

Victor nodded. In the back of his mind he wondered what his estranged daughter, Ana, was doing. She had turned from *Tupay* to *Taqe*. In the Incan legend, the Daughter of Darkness, his daughter, was to wear the assembled Emerald Key Necklace. And if she did, the energy around the earth would shift from heavy *Tupay* energy to light *Taqe* energy. That just couldn't happen! Victor had tried to kill his estranged daughter earlier, but her ability to send him love had sent him running. Ana now worked at the Vesica Pisces Foundation with other Warriors for the Light. What were they planning? He could feel them in a subtle way but couldn't pick up directly on their next steps. That made him wary and anxious. He could never directly face off with his daughter again. Victor was sure that her love for him would utterly destroy him if he allowed such a confrontation to take place. And that wouldn't happen. No, they had to steal this next sphere. That way, he'd have two of the seven spheres and the *Taqe* wouldn't be able to thread the necklace.

As Victor made sure his office was in order, he frowned. Something was up. What was happening at the foundation headquarters outside of Quito, Ecuador? Or was he picking up on a meeting at the *Taqe* stronghold at the Village of the Clouds? Victor was dying to be a fly on the wall to hear the *Taqe* discuss their latest strategy.

"Victor Guerra is getting ready to go to Rosslyn Chapel," Calen told the assembled group at the Vesica Pisces Foundation. Around the table sat the elders who led the Village of the Clouds, Alaria and Adaire. Next to Calen's husband, Reno Manchahi, was Ana Ridfort, the estranged daughter of Guerra. Seated next to her was Mace, her husband. "I had a dream this morning showing me that he and two of his knights are going to possess three humans in that vicinity to keep watch over Mary Anderson and Nicholas de Beaufort."

Ana stirred. Her long black hair hung around her shoulders. "Your dreams are always true. Have you warned Nicholas?"

"Yes," Calen said. She sat at the head of the mahogany oval table in their operations room. "I telepathed the information to him as soon as I awoke."

"Good," Mace said, giving his wife a warm look, "because we know Guerra is going to pull out all the stops to get those last two spheres. They don't know that two spheres are located in the chapel. They think it's only one of them and that's good news for us. If Guerra knew there were two I think he'd bring every *Tupay* knight in the realm to battle us."

Reno gave his wife a concerned look and then focused on the elders from the Village of the Clouds. "I agree with you, Mace. We don't want that kind of ultimate confrontation. Let Guerra think there is only one sphere." He glanced over at Alaria. "Guerra and his knights can't enter the chapel. It's off-limits to them. Right?"

Alaria, dressed in a pale apricot cotton shift, nodded. "That is true. But what we don't know is this—if Guerra and his knights possess these humans will they try to seek entrance into the chapel?" She opened her hands. "You know that when *Tupay* possess humans, the laws about them entering sacred and off-limits *Taqe* spaces become very gray." She looked over at her bearded husband. "Thoughts on this, Adaire?"

"We don't know," Adaire said.

"But Rosslyn is one of our premier *Taqe* sacred areas," Ana protested softly. "And it's guarded by Sophia, the Great Mother Goddess herself. How could she not stop them from entering or from following Mary and Nicholas into the chapel?"

Again, Alaria shrugged. She ran her fingers down one of the silver braids that lay across her shoulders. "We simply don't know, Ana. There are karmic possibilities, but none of us are privy to them. The Great Mother Goddess has her own plans and she's not telling anyone."

"I wish to hell we did know. It would make things easier on us. On Mary and Nicholas," Reno said in a low growl.

Calen reached out and placed her fingers over her Apache husband's forearm. "We know this Emerald Key Necklace is a game-changer in the world. So does Guerra. It's up to humans to decide which they want—to continue as they have for the last five thousand years with heavy energy or to change to the light energy. Ultimately, we who are in human form will make that decision."

Reno smiled at his courageous wife. "As always, your common sense is the real answer."

Ana looked to Mace and then across the table at the elders. "Where does this leave us? We know that Jeff Anderson, who is in the *Tupay* castle, is just waiting for my father and his men to leave for Earth and the third-dimensional plane. He's been in touch with you, Alaria?"

Nodding, the elder said, "Jeff waits and

watches. He intends to steal the sphere at the right moment. He can't steal it too soon or it will tip Guerra off. We want him to go hunt Mary and Nicholas thinking all is well at the castle. I'm in touch with Jeff. He will go to the office on my orders. We are using this ploy as a critical strategy to give Mary and Nicholas room to get the spheres."

"And then we'll come to the village and you'll restring the necklace?" Ana asked.

Adaire nodded. "Yes, as soon as we have all seven emeralds, Alaria will string them together. We have an area being laid out in the center of our village right now for you to stand during the ceremony. Alaria will place the necklace upon you, Ana. After that, we don't know what will happen. It is all up to you."

Ana sighed. "I'm worried about that."

"Don't be, child," Alaria said. "Of all the Warriors for the Light, you are the one seated so powerfully in your heart. Your love will automatically work with this necklace. What will happen, I do not know. But you will be safe and you are the key to all of this."

"Don't forget," Reno reminded them, looking in Mace's direction, "Nicholas comes from a line of Templars and Cathars. There is no accident he's involved in this. The Templars were guardians of the Great Mother Goddess all along. That was their great secret. And Mace Ridfort is a descendant of Gerard de Ridfort, who was a Templar Grand Master from 1191 to 1193. Nicholas and Mace provide the highest *Taqe* warrior energy we have. And it will suffice. I know it will."

Calen wasn't as sure as her Apache husband. She saw the fierceness in his golden-brown eyes. There was nothing passive about Reno. He was a jaguar shape-shifter and a warrior by blood and by heritage. Patting his arm, she said, "The Templars have always upheld the equality of women and men. That is why they continued to hold the light of hope for women during the Dark Ages when they were property and were barely as important as farm animals. We owe the Templars a lot."

She smiled warmly down the table at Mace and Ana. "And now Ana is eight months pregnant with your first child, a child who carries Templar genes and memory. As the Daughter of Darkness, the next in line to rule the *Tupay,* you turned away from your father and his way of life and came to us. When you walked across the bridge into the Village of the Clouds, you became one of us, Ana. If you are allowed to wear the Emerald Key Necklace as a pregnant mother, it will be the most wonderful sign from the Great Mother Goddess that Earth is poised to rebirth itself and those who live upon her."

"Indeed," Adaire said, nodding his head and giving Ana a warm smile. "I pray for the day that Alaria can place that necklace about your neck, Ana. Imagine! This child you carry will be bathed in the light of this powerful energy that is heart-fueled. Your child will be an important turning point for all of us, in all dimensions, if this happens."

Ana gently moved her hand across her swollen belly. "I've given a lot of thought to that," she admitted softly. "I have never felt so much love as I have since I became pregnant. I know all of this has meaning. It is more than a symbol."

"Great Mother Goddess willing," Alaria said, "you have become an archetypal symbol in the flesh for the Earth changes that will occur on December 21, 2012. The Mayan prophecy tells us that time as we know it will cease."

Calen grimaced. "Right now the fearmongers among humans are saying this will be the end of the world. They misunderstand the prophecy. Nothing could be further from the truth."

Alaria nodded. "Those who fear will always interpret something the way they want to see it. Time has been speeding up on Earth since the 1988 harmonic convergence event. People in 2010 are seeing that their choices have immediate consequences. Before, our choices might not come back to haunt us for years or even lifetimes." She opened her hands. "Now, with time speeding up as it has, it means our thoughts and actions have instant, rubber-band-like responses back into our personal lives. That's all."

"A far cry from the end of life on Earth," Calen grumbled.

Everyone chuckled.

"Consider this," Alaria told them. "When one is going to give birth, time ceases. You are in the everpresent now. When you wear the necklace, Ana, the Great Mother will birth the light from her cosmic womb and it will flow like a golden downpouring of compassionate energy throughout our universe."

"Let's hope this energy enfolds the earth," Mace commented.

"It will," Alaria said. "Each person's aura will absorb it." She held up her hands. "However, if a person does not want to be enfolded by this healing heart energy, they can reject it."

"What happens to them then?" Calen wondered.

Adaire's thick white brows rose. "Their lives will be reviewed. Once they see the unhealthy choices they've made, their own heavy energy will dissolve them. Their spirit will be released and they will go to the land of the *Tupay*."

"And those who allow themselves to absorb this higher, refined energy," Alaria added, "will then find themselves feeling more hopeful, desiring peace on Earth and no more wars. As more and more people absorb this released energy, there will be a huge shift toward compassion and service. Heavy energy like hatred, prejudice, war, violence, jealousy, hypocrisy, lying and all the rest of the lower human choices will be lessened."

"I like this idea," Ana said, "that we will once more care for Mother Earth rather than destroying her with air, land and water pollution."

"Right," Adaire said, lifting his eyes toward the ceiling. "And may the Great Mother Goddess finally give us the light and heart we have so desperately needed but not received for the last thirteen thousand years on Earth. And the last five thousand have been the worst and the darkest we've seen in Earth's history."

"It is time for a major shift," Alaria agreed. "The only question is whether the Earth will be showered with continued *Tupay* energy or, if we can get all seven emerald spheres, will it be tilted in the new direction of love, peace and harmony of the *Taqe?*"

Nicholas was facing Mary when he winced. A compression of energy, much like an invisible earthquake, shuddered through him. Mary's eyes widened.

"What was that?" she asked, shaken and looking around his hotel room. "What just happened?"

Nicholas felt every hair on his neck stand up. Instantly, he was at Mary's side. Without thinking, he pulled her into the safety of his arms, every protective alarm within him going off. She moved into his embrace, her body pressed softly against his hard planes. All his focus was on the disturbance in the energy fields. His arms were around her waist and he felt the birdlike beat of her heart against his. "I don't know. Be still. Let me try to find out…"

Nicholas psychically opened up and began to scan the local area. Whatever had happened wasn't good. It was like a sonic boom created by a jet breaking the speed of sound. Only, no one had heard it. People who were psychic and sensitive would feel it, too, but he was doubtful they'd understand or know what they'd felt.

The trembling, shuddering vibrations continued in the invisible realms. It was as if a major earthquake had occurred and now he was feeling the aftershocks. His arms tightened about Mary. Nicholas could smell the sweet lavender of her shampoo and her own alluring scent. Ordinarily, he'd have been distracted, but not now, not with what had just occurred.

Through clenched teeth, Nicholas hissed, "It's the Dark Lord, Victor Guerra. He's just arrived here at Rosslyn with two other knights."

Mary pulled away from Nicholas and looked up into his hard face. "What does that mean? I don't understand."

Nicholas released her but kept hold of her hand. He led her toward the window that over-looked the road, the chapel partly visible in the distance. Many people were coming and going from the chapel, and several tourist buses were parked nearby. "It means that Guerra and his men are here to stalk us, Mary." He narrowed his eyes and shifted his sight so he could see people's auras. Nothing looked out of place, but he knew when a human was possessed, little could be discerned. He explained the process to Mary. When he was done with the explanation, her face went pale.

"I didn't mean to scare you," he said, gentling his tone. Without thinking, he reached out and tamed some of the curls off her creased forehead. "I'm sorry." Her hair was silky as his fingers glided through the tresses. Oh, how badly he wanted to love Mary! His soul mate. His forever love. Some color came to her cheeks as he caressed her hair.

Scalp tingling, Mary felt fear race through her. When Nicholas had touched her, she'd sensed his instant protection. The fierce eagle-like look in his green eyes made her feel safer. "C-could Guerra possess you? Or me?" Mary was more worried for Nicholas than herself. She understood his role in being here with her. Love for him welled up suddenly within her, a desperate love that was as old as time itself. This threat had put her in touch with her fierce bond with this man who stood stalwartly before her. Nicholas squeezed her hand with gentle strength.

"He could try," Nicholas growled. "I'd never allow him or one of his *Tupay* knights to do that to you. I'd kill them." What he left unsaid was that he would die trying. Nicholas would step in front of Mary and take the hit, the possession, instead. She was shaken enough that he didn't want to inflame her fears any more than necessary.

"That's good to know," Mary whispered, her hand against her hard-beating heart. Nicholas was studying the people walking down Chapel Close toward Rosslyn Chapel. "What are you doing? I feel you searching for something."

"I received a telepathic warning this morning from Calen who is living in Quito, Ecuador. She and her husband run the Vesica Pisces Foundation for the *Taqe,*" he said, turning to her. "Last night Calen had a dream." Nicholas told her about it.

"So, you knew Guerra was coming?" Mary thought it wonderful that Calen, whom she'd never met, had had a foretelling dream that would help Nicholas protect her.

"Yes," he replied as he continued to scan the crowds of people. There had to be over a hundred tourists and it would be impossible to see each one's aura from this distance. He'd have to move through the crowd to discover the auras of the three *Tupay*. There were telltale signs, and it was his job to find them. Nicholas couldn't take on three *Tupay,* but he could at least keep an eye on them.

Mary felt the strength in Nicholas's hand around hers. She was just beginning to realize how powerful this man, her soul mate, really was. She knew he was looking for the *Tupay* who had just possessed three unsuspecting people. Were they down there? What would happen to them, now? The questions were many. Suddenly, Mary didn't want to be alone in her room. She needed Nicholas at her side, in her bed, holding her. And when they had to go out, she wanted his hand around hers. For the first time, Mary felt the savage threat as it moved through her in wave after wave. The Dark Lord would come after her once she found the spheres. And he'd kill her to get them.

Chapter 10

"Stay here," Nicholas told Mary. He reluctantly released her hand as they stood looking out the hotel window. He saw the sudden fear in her eyes as he took a step away. It was the last thing he wanted to do. Just holding her inflamed his desire for her, but he made himself walk toward the door. "Don't answer the door, Mary. I'm walking to the chapel grounds to see if I can locate the *Tupay*."

Mary stared at him. "What if you do, Nicholas? What will happen?"

He gave her a grim look. "First, I have to locate them. They're wolves hiding in sheeps' clothing. I may not be able to detect them at all. If the *Tupay* knights and the Dark Lord himself are here, I may not be able to ferret them out. If it's someone of lower rank and training, I might get lucky. It takes a lot of power and skill to hide in a human body and not be discovered by someone like myself."

Placing her hand at her throat, Mary could feel the pulse in her neck. "What if you find them?" she pressed, frightened.

"Then I will try to destroy them as they will try to destroy me," he said.

As her face went pale, Nicholas kicked himself inwardly for being so brusque. While he wanted to go back to her, to give her a calming embrace, he could not. If he had Mary in his arms, he would drag her to his bed and make hot, torrid love with her despite his ancient vow. "Everything will be all right," he soothed. "You have to trust me, Mary."

"I do. I always have."

"I won't fail you," Nicholas murmured, leaving as quietly as a ghost. "Lock the door behind me. I will give you three sharp knocks upon my return."

Nodding, Mary did as he asked.

Nicholas quickly made his way down the carpeted staircase to the street below. In hunting mode, his eyes were narrowed and he switched on his full clairvoyant ability to see individual auras. It was high tourist season at Rosslyn Chapel and at least a hundred people were milling around the entrance to the ancient site.

Thinking that the *Tupay* would not send someone of low rank to try to intercept Mary and him, Nicholas placed a heavy bubble of protection around himself. It would be impossible for the *Tupay* to pick up on his power.

Nicholas crossed the street and quickly walked down the road, aiming for the main entrance to the chapel. After buying a ticket, he sauntered onto the grounds with a brochure. He leaned languidly against the gray stone corner near the west entrance and pretended to be a genuine visitor. It was best to fit in, not to stand out as he scanned the tourists. Now, to hunt for the *Tupay* among all these human beings…

Victor chose his victim. He liked strong young men precisely because of their athletic ability. There might come a time when he would have to use the human's strength. There was a twenty-year-old with red hair and freckles standing off to the side of the crowd. His looks, build and dress marked him as Scottish. Good, this young man had a healthy aura and he was tall and well-muscled. The lad was eagerly studying a map of Rosslyn Chapel beneath the shade trees near the east side. Very few people were at this end. Most were on the west side close to the entrance. As he waited, Victor saw that Lothar and Marcus had also chosen their quarries—a pair of blond English brothers in their twenties. They, too, were apart from the crowd of tourists at the north end, which was almost free of other people.

Telepathically, Victor ordered his knights to possess their unsuspecting victims, then he did the same. Diving down, he smashed into the crown of his victim's head. Instantly, the man dropped the map and gasped. Too late! Victor shot into the man's form and literally squashed the personality of the lad around the physical edges of his body. He inflated himself and was careful not to allow most of his power to enter the body. If he did, it would instantly kill his victim. And right now, Victor wanted the young man alive and functioning. He felt the man's knees soften for a moment. The man, who was called Blaire, struggled mightily against the sudden invasion, but Victor trapped him into such a tight space that all the fight went out of him. Victor pushed an energy hook into the young man's brain. All the information about him flowed into Victor. Now, Victor could hide under the guise of Blaire with all his knowledge, language and education. Blaire was a university student studying archeology. And he'd come to Rosslyn Chapel because he was writing a paper on Gothic sculptures. *Perfect!* He'd done well to choose this Scot.

Through Blaire's eyes, Victor saw that his knights had possessed the two English brothers. Waving at them, Victor indicated that they should thread through the crowds and make their way over to where he stood. When they arrived, Victor spoke in a low voice that couldn't be heard by others.

"Problems?"

"None," Marcus replied. "This boys' name is Stephen."

"And I'm Lawrence," Lothar said. He gave Victor a silly grin.

"Good," Victor said. "Now, for the important things. Let's nose around the chapel grounds. There's a talk by a guide within the chapel that we should hear. Providing we can get into the chapel at all. We know Sophia is the guardian here. The real question is whether she will allow us inside as possessed humans."

Lothar slicked his fingers through the thick, curly blond hair of Lawrence. "We have to try. If we can get inside this *Taqe* sacred site, all the better for us."

Grunting, Victor agreed. He felt Blaire struggling again and applied a little more force to the spirit of the man to make him settle down. Some spirits were strong and struggled off and on, particularly in the first hour after possession. Blaire was not only strong physically, but he had a powerful spirit, too. "Let's split up. I'll try to enter the chapel in a bit. If I make it in, then you follow. First, I want to scan this crowd and see if there's a *Taqe* warrior on the premises before we do anything else."

As Victor settled more comfortably into Blaire's body, he quickly scanned the jovial and eager crowd. He noted people from around the world here to view this chapel. His interest, however, was not in them as much as their auras. Silver in an aura showed the person was *Taqe.* Whether the person was a warrior still had to be determined. People seeking light and spiritual evolvement always had some silver, usually a little, but it was there nonetheless.

Leaning against a chestnut tree, the sun hidden by the leaves, Victor intently scanned the crowd. There were women, children, babies and men. They came in all colors. Young, middle-aged and old. Yes, Rosslyn Chapel's call was a mighty beacon to *Taqe* people, no doubt, and that made Victor unhappy.

Suddenly, Victor felt the energy change, as if a ripple had begun on a quiet pond's surface. He knew that feeling. A powerful Warrior for the Light had just arrived! Where was he? Craning his neck, Victor tried to absorb more auras. Whoever it was, he was powerful, almost as powerful as himself. That made Victor nervous. Few *Taqe* could meet his four thousand years of accumulated power, but he knew there was a handful out there who could. One of Victor's dark secrets was his fear of being killed by just such a mighty *Taqe* warrior.

Where was this *Taqe?* Was he in spirit and not body? Victor didn't know. His heart started a slow pound of dread. Even worse, did the warrior know of him? The cat-and-mouse game had begun once more for Victor.

Nicholas remained at the corner of the chapel pretending to be a tourist. People were chatting amiably with one another as they waited their turns to enter the chapel. The hair on his neck stood up, always a sign of *Tupay* nearby. Scanning the people in the crowd, he looked for a bright or lurid red color in their auras. When a *Tupay* assaulted a human, the human's aura showed the shock of sudden possession, and the healthy reds turned a darkish-brown or murky red color.

Nicholas's heart started a slow, warning pound. *There.* He saw two young blond men coming around from the front of the chapel toward him and the west entrance. Carefully, Nicholas scanned their auras. Each had a dirty red in it. A warning went off in Nicholas as he burned their faces into his memory. As he continued to scan the tourists, he felt a sense of uncertainty. Behind the two men were a husband and wife. They, too, had dirty red colors in their auras. They were arguing with one another in quiet, intense tones. Ahead of the two blonds were five college guys. Their auras also sported brownish-reds.

Mouth quirking, Nicholas wondered if Victor Guerra had sent an entire company of *Tupay* knights to Rosslyn Chapel. Were all of the auras he saw on humans possessed by these knights? Unsure, he continued to study the people. At one point, he sauntered over to one of the benches and sat down to get a better view of the only entrance/exit point to the chapel. Resuming his tourist cover, Nicholas opened the brochure and pretended to study it. He had to fit in with the crowd, not stand out like a gawker staring at everyone. From time to time, he'd look up and watch the blond men as they ambled around the yard.

His gut told him those two were *Tupay* knights. There was nothing he could do but earmark them. He needed to wait and see if they became aggressive. Or if they wandered over to the hotel in search of Mary, who was their real target. The two blonds looked ill, and they didn't speak as they walked toward the entrance. They looked out of place in the amiable crowd.

Had the arrival of these two sent that wave of warning to Nicholas? Unsure, he continued to scan. Buses came and went, loading and unloading tourists. There was an air of anticipation and happiness in the crowd, Nicholas observed. He didn't blame the people because walking into Rosslyn Chapel was like getting bathed in high, loving energy. A healing could occur if the person was open to it. If not, they still came away with a sense of lightness, joy and hope.

Such was high *Taqe* light energy. And Rosslyn Chapel was truly a world beacon of *Taqe* light, which explained why so many people were coming here. It didn't hurt that author Dan Brown, who penned *The Da Vinci Code,* had written a book and highlighted Rosslyn Chapel. That is why so many visitors were coming to see it with their own eyes. Brown had done the world a positive service.

Suddenly, Nicholas became more attentive. A third lad, a redhead, approached the two blonds. His aura, too, held that dirty red streak. The redhead was pointing toward the village of Roslin where Mary had stayed in the hotel. One of the blonds left and started walking toward Roslin. Something was up. Careful not to draw attention to himself, Nicholas stood and was ready to act. His heart pounded with dread. Remaining inconspicuous, Nicholas followed him for the short walk on the narrow Chapel Close and across the street to the hotel.

Nicholas moved inside the hotel and past the man. The blond stood at the registration desk impatiently waiting for the woman clerk to get off the phone. Nicholas took the stairs to the third floor. Was he trying to find Mary? Was he asking the clerk about Mary?

*   *   *

Mary sat on a chair near the desk in Nicholas's room. She was bored, but anxious. Her own clairvoyant skills were on and she could feel tension in the air. She wished for the hundredth time that Nicholas and she shared telepathic abilities.

There was a soft knock on the door.

"Maid service," the male voice cheerfully announced.

Mary shot to her feet. She'd put the dead bolt on the door. Rushing to it, she called out, "I don't want any towels today, thank you."

Her heart skittered with fear. She felt the aura of the man on the other side. Something was wrong. What was it?

"Fresh towels," the male voice insisted more strongly.

Now she was afraid. Mary backed away from the door, her hand on the base of her throat. "I don't want any!" she shouted. "Go away!"

Nicholas was out of breath as he slipped through the door at the end of the hall. *Damn!* He saw the blond knocking on the door to his room. This was a *Tupay!* Mouth flattening, Nicholas raced down the hall toward him. It was kill or be killed.

Marcus suddenly heard a pounding sound coming toward him. Jerking his head to the right, he saw a tall, angular man with a warrior's face hurtling toward him. He had no time to turn. In an instant, Marcus was thrown off his feet. A fist balled and came at him. His head exploded, his nose broke. Pain filled Marcus as he struggled to get the upper hand. The rage in the *Taqe*'s eyes was fearsome. Marcus wasn't afraid, but he knew he should be as the man's hands wrapped around his neck and squeezed.

And then, Marcus felt a new energy flooding into the human he'd possessed. No! Instantly, Marcus fled out of the body and disappeared into the fourth dimension. He didn't stop until he'd blipped back into the safety of the *Tupay* castle. He felt his body shuddering. Angry over the unexpected attack, Marcus quickly got into contact with the Dark Lord.

Victor listened to the telepathic message. He was standing near the entrance to Rosslyn Chapel with Lothar. After hearing the message, he snarled a curse beneath his breath. Glaring over at Lothar, he telepathed, *Get rid of this body now! Find a new one! A* Taqe *Warrior for the Light just attacked Marcus. Worse, this warrior has superior powers. He sent love energy into the body Marcus possessed. He had to flee or die.*

Lothar gulped and bobbed his head. *Yes, my lord.* Quickly, he eased away from the onlookers and walked around the edge of the chapel where he could not be seen.

Victor cursed again. *This isn't good,* he told Marcus.

No, it isn't, my lord. I'm sorry I could not defeat him.

Victor worried about that. No one had ever won a fight with Marcus—until just now. *Who is he?*

I don't know, my lord.

In your opinion, is he as strong as I am? Victor felt his stomach clench in fear over the answer.

He took me like a rank beginner to war, my lord. Once he had me on the floor and willed that loving energy into the body, I knew his superior power.

The only energy in the universe that could kill a *Tupay*'s spirit was the energy of love. The one thing *Tupay* refused to do was to move into their heart chakra to practice compassion and peace. *Tupay* were ruled by immature, primitive human emotions by the lower three chakras. Victor realized he had to switch to another body.

Leaving the line, Victor walked around to the rear of Rosslyn Chapel on the north side. There, he pulled out of the human named Blaire, zoomed out of his head and back into the fourth dimension. As soon as he exited Blaire's body, the youth collapsed and died five minutes later. Feeling no remorse, Victor remained in the fourth dimension and began the hunt for another human body. The police or some bystander would eventually stumble upon Blaire's dead body.

He'd ordered Lothar to take the human he'd possessed to the glen and exit the body in the V-shaped canyon of woodlands down below the hill where Rosslyn Chapel stood. There, the body would not be found for some time. Victor couldn't have a bunch of dead human bodies littering the chapel grounds or there would be police all over the place, and that would complicate their mission. Damn that *Taqe* warrior!

Mary leaped to her feet as she heard three sharp knocks on the door. Earlier, there'd been a scuffle outside the thick wooden door, but she hadn't wanted to investigate. This time she shakily approached the door and pressed her hands against it.

"Nicholas?" she called, her voice trembling.

"It's me," he said sharply, "open up."

Unlocking the dead bolt, she saw him standing grimly before her. His black hair was mussed, and there were scratches on his hands. The knuckles on his right hand were swollen.

"Oh, God, what happened?" she asked, standing aside for him to enter.

"Shut the door and lock it," he told her tersely, moving to the bathroom. There, he turned on the water, washed his hands, combed his hair and wiped away the sweat from his face.

Mary slid the dead bolt and moved to the open door of the bathroom. "Something terrible happened. I felt it."

Nodding, he wiped his face with the towel. In as few words as possible, he told Mary everything. There was no sense in hiding the truth from her.

"We're being hunted by the *Tupay*," were her words as she stood back and he exited the bathroom.

"Yes."

"What did you do with the body of that poor young man?"

"I carried him down to the basement. They'll find him there. When the doctor performs an autopsy on him, he'll find he died of a heart attack."

"They won't suspect us?"

Shaking his head, Nicholas pulled off his polo shirt to reveal his broad, deep chest. "No. I need a shower." He wanted all evidence of the scuffle erased. Glancing up, he saw Mary standing by the other side of the bed.

"What do you want me to do?" She was unsure whether to stay or not. Despite the fear and threat, she thought Nicholas looked magnificent standing before her partially clothed. Dark hair covered his chest. He had two blade scars on his torso. His shoulders were broad. Every muscle moved smoothly into the next as he tossed the towel on the bed. His eyes grew feral when he noticed her appreciative gaze.

"After I shower, I'm going to throw these clothes away. I'll get changed and then we'll both go to your room and collect your things. You'll stay here, with me. In this room."

"Are—you sure?" Mary suddenly felt a powerful desire rifle through her like a fierce storm. The idea of sharing this beautiful room with Nicholas was tantalizing. Teasing. How was she going to handle her emotions? All Mary wanted was to love Nicholas, to once more join with him. Sophia's words and her pronouncement that she had to make love with Nicholas came back to her.

Nicholas was never more sure than now. Mary's eyes went wide, her lips parted, and inwardly he groaned. Cursing the *Tupay,* he hated that they had been forced into this situation. He couldn't leave Mary unguarded now that they were being actively searched for. "We don't have a choice," he growled. He moved to the bathroom and closed the door. What he wanted to do was invite Mary in with him. They could shower together…and what about his ancient vow?

Mary sat down, her eyes never leaving the closed door. Her hands were damp as she clenched them in her lap. Looking around the room, bright with late-afternoon light, she sighed. All of a sudden her quiet, happy life had evaporated. She would be stuck in a room with a man who made her ache so deeply she wondered if she had the strength to continue resisting him. Or to honor his vow from his last life.

There was only one large bed in the room. How would they sleep? Mary couldn't trust herself if she shared that bed with Nicholas. And yet, it was the one thing she wanted most: him. Mary wanted to love Nicholas, to once more reconnect with him, to absorb his maleness within her. Yes, that was what she wanted. Even with all the danger swirling around them, Mary realized how ancient her desire for Nicholas really was.

The real question was: What did Nicholas want?

Chapter 11

After showering, Nicholas toweled off and pulled on a fresh set of clothes. His mind was whirling with plans. Steam filtered out the open door as he emerged. Mary was sitting on the chair near the desk. She seemed preoccupied.

"Come on," he told her gruffly, "we have to leave. The *Tupay* know we're here."

"Where can we go?" Mary asked, distress evident in her voice.

"We'll find something. Come on, I'll escort you to your room and you can pack your bags."

By the time they left in a taxi, it was evening.

Nicholas was fully on guard. The crowds were gone from Rosslyn Chapel. The quaint Scottish town of Roslin was once more quiet. And deadly, Mary decided as she slipped into the taxi's backseat with Nicholas. She heard him give the address of a popular bed-and-breakfast about ten minutes away in an area known as Midlothian.

The sky had turned a beautiful red and orange as the sun set across the rolling green hills. The taxi pulled up to the Hillwood Bed and Breakfast, where they had a stunning view of the rolling green Pentland Hills at the front of the property. To the rear sat the Moorfoot Hills. Surrounded by farmland, the B and B looked completely inviting and safe to Mary. It was a whitewashed house set against a pastoral landscape. Turrets sat at each corner of the front of the slate-roofed home. In front, curved doors and red brick created a welcoming entrance. Even in the dusk, Mary appreciated the beauty that surrounded the three-story home. Nicholas paid the cabbie, got out and took their bags from the trunk. They were met by a young woman named Edana Reid, the daughter of the owners. She smiled and warmly welcomed them to the B and B.

Within no time, they were in their suite, the

Finlay Room. They accepted the hot tea and scones from Edana, but gently refused to sit with her in the large room with the fireplace. Instead, Nicholas carried the tray with the food and tea to their room. Edana accepted his reason—they'd just gotten off a flight, were terribly jet-lagged and wanted to go to bed early.

The Finlay Room was huge, painted a clean white with pleasant blue and green appointments. Mary stared at the king-size bed. There was only one bed. Nicholas had wanted a room on the first floor with a door that would lead to the outside. Mary understood why. If they were attacked by the *Tupay,* he wanted two ways to escape. The seriousness of their mission depressed her. Her dream of finding the beautiful emerald spheres had turned into a real nightmare.

After Nicholas had paid for the room, he returned and slid the dead bolt into position on the door. Mary was dutifully unpacking her suitcase but her expression was one of anxiety. Nicholas took a deep breath, itching to place his hands on her small shoulders to comfort her.

Looking up, Mary managed a slight smile. "I was just thinking that my dream of finding the spheres has turned into a real-life nightmare," she admitted, keeping her voice low.

Nodding, Nicholas leaned against the door, his arms crossed. If he didn't hold himself back, he'd break his sworn oath and go over and embrace Mary, kiss her and drag her off to that beautiful bed. "It's not easy for someone like yourself. You're not trained in psychic warfare or combat."

"No…I'm not," she said, folding her only sweater and walking over to the dresser drawer.

"I'm sorry, Mary. I can see you're upset. This isn't what you signed on for."

Quietly shutting the drawer, she turned and studied him as he rested almost languidly against the door, his arms across his chest. No matter how she saw Nicholas, the warrior-monk in him stared back at her. His oval face and high cheekbones only accentuated his large but narrowed green eyes. She imagined him in his white tunic with the bright red cross on it over his chain mail. "I didn't know what I was sign-ing up for," she admitted in jest. Walking to the bed where her suitcase sat open, she picked up some of her socks. "This is life or death. That's shocking. I had no idea that there was a real bat-tle going on in the fourth dimension between the heavy and light energy forces."

Nicholas had tried his best to bring Mary up

to speed on what "else" was out there, things that most people in the third dimension were never aware of. Just because they didn't know about it didn't mean it wasn't happening. "Try to focus on the fact that you were chosen by the Great Mother Goddess to retrieve the last two emerald spheres. That says so much about your heart, Mary." And oh, how Nicholas wanted to show her how much he loved her and had always loved her. He wasn't at all surprised that the Great Mother had chosen her. Mary's heart was as pure as the clear stream that ran through the glen behind Rosslyn Chapel.

Shutting her emptied suitcase, Mary placed it in the closet. "I try to, Nicholas. You have to appreciate that all my life, I've been involved in quilting, designing and giving lectures. Not running around on a life-or-death mission."

Smiling sourly, Nicholas relaxed and his arms fell to his sides. Outside the window, the sky was turning orange. He liked the energy of this B and B. Here, he felt somewhat safe. "It's a lot to handle," he admitted.

Standing on the other side of the king-size bed, Mary said, "What do we do now?" She gestured to the bed. "There's only one bed."

Nicholas fought against the desire that begged

to be torn from his lips. Instead, he said, "You take the bed. I'll sleep on the floor near the door. There're extra blankets and pillows in the closet."

"But…the floor?"

Hearing the distress in her voice, he held up his hand. "Mary, I'm used to sleeping on hard floors and the earth. I don't own a bed at the Village of the Clouds. I prefer a pallet on hard-packed earth. It's what I was used to in my last incarnation as a Templar knight. Don't worry, it's not uncomfortable."

Shrugging, Mary murmured, "Okay…"

"Why don't you get a shower? Or a bath?"

Mary agreed and went to the bathroom. She had already hung her light blue knee-length cotton shirt on the hook. Without a word, she quietly shut the door. The bathroom was large and scrupulously clean. The bathtub called to her and she leaned over and turned on the faucets. What would tonight bring? An attack? Harm to them? She shuddered, unsure.

Where are they? Victor stood in the dusky glen below Rosslyn Chapel. The gray Gothic walls gleamed orange in the colorful sunset. He'd come back into the third dimension and possessed a local young man who worked as a guide at Rosslyn Chapel, and then Victor had begun to sense out the location of the two *Taqe*. He'd retraced his knight's steps over to the Original Roslin Inn. By questioning the staff, he'd found out two people had left an hour ago—Mary Anderson and Nicholas de Beaufort. The woman behind the mahogany desk at the hotel said she did not know where they'd gone. After digging into her mind, Victor discovered she was correct. The woman had gone pale and crumpled in her chair as he viciously sorted through her memories. He left her with a migraine headache.

Victor ordered Lothar to remain in the fourth dimension for the time being. *Taqe* left energy trails and he ordered Lothar to try to locate their trail. Lothar reported back that their trail had been erased. Standing in the glen, Victor held on to his rage. The Templar knight had dispatched one of his oldest and dearest friends, Marcus. And he'd done it swiftly and efficiently. Marcus had fled the possessed body before it was too late. The loving compassion the *Taqe* had sent into Marcus had almost destroyed his spirit. It had been too close a call for his Roman-soldier friend.

Victor understood that this was one hell of a confrontation. Each time he went after another sphere, the *Taqe* raised the ante with qualified warriors. If he couldn't get the emerald sphere here at Rosslyn, it would be awful. True, he had one sphere and that would stop the *Taqe* from stringing the necklace and placing it around his estranged daughter's neck. Hate and bitterness flowed through Victor as he thought of Ana, his only daughter. Oh, it was true that he'd killed Ana's mother by pushing her off a cliff in Peru while she was carrying his daughter. Out in the wild of that night, Ana had been born, and a female jaguar had come, had carried the newborn off in her mouth and back to her lair to be raised in the wilds of the Peruvian jungle.

Angrily, Victor glared at Rosslyn Chapel, now in silhouette as the night moved silently across the Scottish sky. Would the Great Mother Goddess allow him entrance into that sacred shrine of the *Taqe* tomorrow morning? Victor didn't know, but he'd give it a try as a guide. At least if he could get inside, he could energetically try to sniff out the sphere.

As the stars began to wink and play in the dark sky above him, Victor shivered. Edinburgh sat near the North Sea and the ocean's dampness came in with the descending darkness. Turning on his heel, Victor walked to where Cameron

Lindsay, the lad he had possessed, lived. He knew the twenty-year-old attended the University of Edinburgh and being a guide at the chapel was a part-time job for him. Well, from now on, Victor would put the lad into a full-time position at Rosslyn, providing he could access the chapel tomorrow morning. Lindsay lived with his parents just six blocks away from the chapel in the village of Roslin. The parents would not know a thing. They wouldn't realize their beloved son had been possessed by the Lord of Darkness.

Mary slept deeply. The day's events had bludgeoned her emotionally and escaping into sleep was the only way to heal her anxious state. Her dreams were colorful, they always were. But this time, they turned lurid, too. Mary found herself in Rosslyn Chapel. She was descending into the crypt, where all the St. Clairs and Sinclairs were entombed after their deaths. Feeling threatened, she peered down into the gloom. The stairs were made of yellow sandstone and below she peered into the empty crypt, the floor blackened from much use. A sense of dread overwhelmed her.

Suddenly, the face of a pale man swooped up from the crypt and came toward her. His eyes were dead and he sported a black-and-gray goatee. Mary felt his desire to invade and possess her. She screamed and fell back against the hard, unyielding stone steps. *No! No!* His thin mouth twisted as he hovered close to her, looking her over. When his hand materialized out of the darkness, the fingers and nails like talons, she shrieked for help.

Nicholas was sleeping lightly, stretched out across the dead-bolted door. As they'd bedded down for the night, he'd drawn a circle of protection around them. The circle acted like an energy alarm to Nicholas. If anyone tried to touch it, he would instantly awake and go on full defensive mode to protect Mary and himself. Her shriek jolted him awake.

Without thinking, Nicholas, dressed only in a set of boxer shorts, leaped up from his pallet and in her direction. Moonlight spilled in through the slats of the venetian blinds. Mary was tearing madly at her covers, caught up in some terrible dream.

"Mary!" he rasped, getting to her side. "Mary!" He reached out to touch her. She was perspiring, sobbing, her eyes wild and haunted. Nicholas eased onto the bed and pulled her into his arms. Sobs tore raggedly from her lips.

"It's all right," he said gruffly, her hair tickling

his chin and cheek. "You're safe, Mary. It's all right. I'm here. I'll protect you...."

Nicholas's soft words barely broke through her terror. She felt the hard warmth of his male body crushing her to him. His arms were like steel bands, nearly binding her as he held her protectively within his embrace. Closing her eyes, Mary reached out, her hand opening and closing against the taut, warm flesh of his chest.

"Oh, Nicholas," she cried. "I saw him! He tried to get me. It was horrible," she choked.

Tears marred her wide eyes. Nicholas automatically ran his hand through her mussed black hair and then down the slope of her spine. The thin cotton nightgown did nothing to hide her lush curves, which he tried to ignore. "Do you know who he was?" he rasped near her ear. His mind spun. One part of him was already testing his line of protection. No one had entered it. Nicholas knew the Dark Lord and what he looked like. Somehow he'd been able to invade Mary's dreams.

Sobbing, Mary shared the nightmare. Nicholas's arms tightened momentarily around her when she was finished. Now she felt safe and protected. There was a fierce defensive energy swirling around Nicholas and she thirstily absorbed his maleness and all that it meant to her. "Who is he? What is he?" she whispered unsteadily, pulling back enough to gaze up into his dark eyes.

"That was Victor Guerra, the Dark Lord of the *Tupay,*" he admitted unwillingly. How had Guerra gotten to Mary? He had the line of protection up. Without thinking, Nicholas leaned down and kissed Mary's curls. Nicholas had no way to figure out how Guerra had found her and then invaded her dream state. This couldn't happen! Again, he kissed her hair in an effort to calm her.

Moaning, Mary turned her head. Instead of his lips touching her hair, they grazed her open mouth. Instantly, she felt Nicholas freeze. Driven by fear, Mary pressed her mouth to his. At first, he didn't move. But then, she felt a rumble, like an earth tremor, from within him, and her world turned into melting heat. His mouth plundered hers hungrily and she found herself returning his ardor with equal measure. At last! He was kissing her, holding her. Mary burrowed herself into Nicholas in every possible way. It drove out the terror, the hatred and predator-like Victor Guerra's presence.

Her hands flattened against his chest, her fingers trailing and tangling through the dark hair across it. His mouth commanded hers with hunger and exploration. At no time did Nicholas hurt her. She felt him monitoring his strength against her. No, there was such seeking exploration and tenderness as his mouth slid across hers, his tongue searching and asking for entrance. She trembled violently in response.

Mary twisted around, her knees beside his long, hard thighs, her breasts pressed flat against his chest. Her arms slid around his broad shoulders; her fingers caressed his thick neck and tangled into his hair. He smelled of maleness, of strength, of fire. The moment she pressed her breasts against his naked chest, her nipples hardened. A moan came from her as he framed her face and drank from her like a dying man in a desert who had just found the well of life. His breathing was torn, flowing across her face, and she inhaled it with an eagerness she'd never felt in her own life. Nicholas was her life! In those moments as his hands gripped her gown and tore it from her body, Mary drowned in his arms.

Nicholas brought Mary onto her back on the bed. She was naked, the moonlight softly accentuating her body, the nipples of her rounded breasts calling to him. Mary's luminous gaze clung to his. She opened her arms to bring him into her embrace. With one swift motion, Nicholas got rid of the boxer shorts. She stared at his arousal and a smile of welcome blossomed across her soft mouth. In that moment, Nicholas realized that his oath from the past was exactly that—from his past. At some point he would go through the pain of breaking it, but not right now. He knew he could choose the time and place when that had to happen.

Moving languidly, like a consummate predator, he slid down upon Mary. As his flesh barely skimmed hers, a wild tingling sensation rolled through him. Groaning, Nicholas felt her arms embrace him, their cool softness against his harder, roughened sunburned flesh. She drew him down upon her, her legs capturing him. He wasn't surprised by her need of him—he was equally starved for her. As he eased his weight upon her curved body, a groan of satisfaction emerged like a growl from his throat. Mary's legs tangled with his, and she raised her hips in invitation. An explosion of joy rippled within him. Nicholas had wanted to touch her, tease her, love her slowly, but all that vaporized as he felt himself sliding into her deep, tight confines. Her lips wreaked fire upon his mouth, cheek, chin and neck. Her hips thrust upward, not taking no for an answer. Within seconds, he felt like an animal caught up in the frenzy of mating.

Scorching fire rose up through Nicholas. He tore his mouth from hers, leaned to capture a taut nipple between his teeth. A cry of pleasure rippled out of her and it sang through his heaving body. Her restless fingers opened and closed frantically against his shoulders. She might have surprised him and captured him, but Nicholas swore he would give her as much pleasure as she bestowed upon him.

In seconds, he raised his head. Lips drawing away from his clenched teeth, head raised upward, his body grew taut as a stretched bow. The fire of orgasm showered through him like an erupting volcano. At the same moment, Mary's climax joined his and together they clung to one another, cries of joy mingling as their bodies celebrated their coming together once more.

Time slowed. Much later, Nicholas moved onto his side and gently drew her against him. They lay facing one another, still joined, with their hearts pounding and arms wrapped around one another. Mary clung to him, her brow against his chin. Her body spasmed and orgasmed again and again as he continued to thrust into her. Each time, it was like an electrical current flowing throughout her lower body and shooting upward. She felt light, joyous and loved. Never had she been so well loved as now. Nicholas was her lover, always had been and always would be. The real world ceased to exist. Mary was only aware of Nicholas in all his strength and maleness, his arms around her and cradling her.

Pressing small kisses along Mary's hairline, Nicholas felt her collapse against him. He absorbed the beauty of their mutual love. Her brow was damp, her black curls silky against his seeking lips. With one hand, he stroked her back and trailed his fingertips down the expanse. Reveling in Mary's warmth, he felt her flesh become goose bumps wherever he caressed her. Little mews of pleasure whispered from her lips. Nicholas smiled into the moonlit room and closed his eyes. At last, he was content. The woman he loved more than anything was in his arms once more. Where she belonged...

Chapter 12

Nicholas smoothed Mary's black hair at her temple, his gaze locked on hers. There was such happiness shining in her eyes. The soft smile on her lips made his heart soar. His fingers trailed down the side of her face, and he cupped her jaw. Leaning over, he placed his mouth tenderly upon hers. He absorbed her feminine scent, the tickle of her curls against his face. He cherished her lips. Mary's arm slid up across his shoulder and pulled him against her. Already, he could feel the renewed surge strengthening him once more to make love with her. Such was the power of the love Nicholas held for his soul mate.

Easing away, Nicholas smiled into her half-closed eyes, drowsy with satisfaction. "I will never get enough of you, beloved."

"Me, neither," Mary admitted in a whisper. Framing his face, she drowned in his green eyes that now glittered with gold. This man was a complete warrior and yet, he was the most tender of lovers with her. Mary felt her body singing beneath the cascade of orgasms she'd experienced a half hour ago. Even now, the heat and throbbing renewed itself within her. She wanted Nicholas again and judging from the hardness pressed against her belly, he felt the same.

"Do you recall any of our lives together?" he murmured against her cheek, inhaling her scent. Nicholas knew that most people did not remember. Once soul mates were brought together again in another incarnation, however, there was such a powerful draw that they were like magnets, unable ever to part from one another in that life.

Nuzzling his jaw and neck, Mary whispered, "No. Does it matter?"

He chuckled against her silky hair, and shook his head. "What matters is that we are here with one another," he said against her small ear. "That is all that is important."

Moving her hips against his, she smiled. "I've

never been so drawn to a man as to you, Nicholas. I don't know why. I only know that I ache for you minute by minute. Is that how it is with you?" Mary lifted her head away to drown once again within his brilliant green gaze. His mouth pulled into a wry smile.

"You're a twenty-four-hour-a-day aphrodisiac to me, beloved. Since meeting you, I have felt this call to be one with you." His brows drifted downward. "I tried to ignore you." Mary reached up and brushed her fingers along his cheek where the sword scar lay. The tingles and heat spread rapidly and Nicholas closed his eyes, savoring her caress.

"I finally understood that my vow from that last life was in the past," he told her. "I allowed myself to release that life and all its suffering. When we get past this mission, I intend to work with Alaria in clearing the trauma from it once and for all." He gazed deeply into her eyes. "The past is the past. We're here. This is another lifetime. And I finally realized all of that, Mary. That was why I could give myself permission to love you."

"I'm so glad, Nicholas," she whispered, sliding her hand across his jaw and cheek. "I saw you wrestling with it, the pain it was causing you. Thank you for having the courage to do this—for us."

He kissed the tip of her nose. "Love has a way of helping stubborn donkeys like myself get on with things." They laughed softly with one another.

"Nicholas…about my dream and the Dark Lord. Do you think he's tied in to me? Am I somehow connected with him because of that dream?"

He shook his head. "No. Being able to enter a person's dream is only that. He's found you through the dream state, but there's nothing else he can do. He knows what you look like now, that's all. He won't be able to do it again. I've put extra protection in place to stop him if he tries it again." He caressed her cheek. "You're safe in your dreams now."

Sighing, Mary absorbed his hard, lean body against her own softer one. She was hills, curves, valleys and mountains compared to his angular and powerful body. It felt so right to her: softness against hardness. Cherishing his embrace, she threaded her fingers through his short black hair. "I feel like a starving animal keening for my mate."

Nicholas smiled and planted a series of kisses

from her brow down her jaw to her lips. "You are my mate. Forever."

The word resonated powerfully within Mary's heart as she met his mouth. There was such restraint; he checked his strength and showered her with his tenderness, instead. The combination did nothing but make her heart sing as she relished the taste and texture of his lips.

Nicholas eased away, knowing that their time was limited. Right now, they were safe because the *Tupay* hadn't found them—yet. Gathering her into his arms, he rested his back against the headboard. Mary was content to lie across him, her head against his left shoulder as he held her. He didn't want to break the enchantment and magic of the moment.

Mary rubbed his neck and shoulder. "What is it, Nicholas? I can feel you're worried about something." Looking up through her lashes, she saw him grimace.

"I can't hide anything from you, can I?" he teased, cupping her jaw and absorbing her shining blue gaze. He had made her happy. She was satiated. Nothing made him more joyous.

"Something happened when we loved one another," Mary murmured. "Sophia wanted us to come together. She didn't say why. I wonder if this is why? I can pick up on your feelings very easily now. Before, I couldn't."

"Sophia is the mother to all of us," Nicholas said, "and she knows best." Nicholas wondered why he'd fought against loving Mary. He understood that his vow in his last life as a Templar did not really carry over to this incarnation. That realization freed him in a way that showered him with immense relief. Above all, Nicholas was a knight-monk and he'd die before he broke a vow.

Nodding, Mary was content to remain in the circle of his arms. She played her fingers through the dark, curling hair across his massive chest. Beneath her palm, she could feel the powerful, steady beat of his heart. "When she told me it meant more than I realized. Perhaps symbolically? I don't know. Do you?"

Nicholas shook his head. "I don't know, either. Sophia is allowing us, for whatever reason, to explore our renewed connection with one another."

"Does it have a bearing on finding the spheres, Nicholas?"

Shrugging, he said, "I don't know. We'll have to wait and see." As he looked around, he added, "For tonight, we're safe. I don't know what Victor Guerra will do next. He *will* do something."

"Tomorrow, we need to go to the chapel, Nicholas. I'm hoping I'll have a dream or something that will tell me where to go, what to do next."

After easing her out of his arms and sliding off the bed, he held out his hand to her. "Your dreams never lead you wrong. Let's take a shower together. I can run my hands over your body and burn it into my soul once more. Then, we'll sleep within one another's arms as it was meant to be."

As she took his hand, nothing seemed more right to Mary than this moment. When his scarred fingers wrapped around hers and he drew her gently off the bed, it was so easy to move up against his taut, lean body. "I like the idea of a shower together, my dearest heart…."

Mary awoke slowly. For a moment, she could not remember where she was. The first thought that came stealing through her sleep-fogged mind was the long, delicious shower with Nicholas the evening before. Even now, her lower body throbbed with heat and the memory of making love within the steamy confines. He'd lifted her against him as if she were a feather. She remembered sliding downward and absorbing him within her needy, waiting body. She'd lost count of the orgasms as the water had created a misty womb of heat and desire around them. Nicholas had carried her out of the shower. She could barely stand, her body vibrating with such lush sensations afterward.

Smiling softly, her eyes still closed, Mary lay on her back, the covers up to her shoulders. Nicholas lay nearby, his arm across her waist in sleep. Then, a dream she'd had came back to her as fog dissolves before the rising sun. This was how it always happened to her; she would move from sleep to this state of not quite being awake yet. Mary saw the pictures gel before her. After they had finished, she opened her eyes. Looking to the left, she saw sunlight peeking in around the window and venetian blinds.

Nicholas stirred, and his arm tightened around Mary's waist. As he opened his eyes, he inhaled the sweet, honey-like scent that was Mary alone. She turned and faced him, a soft smile of welcome on her lips. Leaning forward, he brushed her mouth with his. "Good morning, beloved."

"It is, isn't it?" Mary sighed, sipping kisses from his smiling mouth. Heart singing, she was happy to be pulled into his arms once more, her body pliant against his. She leaned up, her lips barely touching his. "I love you, Nicholas de Beaufort. I love you with my life…."

His heart exploded with such a fierce passion for Mary that he crushed her against him, his mouth commandingly taking hers. For a moment, they lingered in the bliss of their uttered love for one another. Nothing was more poignant, more important to Nicholas than having his soul mate in his arms. *Forever*.

Breathless, Nicholas withdrew from her wet, soft mouth. Her eyes burned with love for him. He felt it through every cell in his body. Moving his fingers gently, he smoothed away the black curls near her temple. "My love for you transcends all time, Mary. It always will."

Embracing him, Mary pulled out of his arms, even though she didn't want to. Sitting up, the covers pooled around her waist, she gloried in his gaze as she sat naked before him. Her breasts tingled and automatically, the nipples hardened beneath the predatory look he gave her. Holding out her hand, she placed it on his shoulder. "I had a dream. I think it's important, Nicholas. I want to share it with you…."

Victor waited just outside the chapel's entrance. He was impatient for the doors to be opened by Maude, an old woman who was hobbling on her cane down the walk toward the locked west door. Would Sophia, the guardian of this sacred *Taqe* space, allow him into Rosslyn or not? It was dicey. Victor had come up against the Great Mother Goddess only twice before in the four thousand years he'd been Dark Lord of the *Tupay*. She had far more power than him. And he respected it. Victor knew that Sophia, an effigy of the creatoress of them all, was neutral when it came to the affairs of humans on Earth. She did not interfere. Would she now?

Posing as the youth who was a guide and lecturer, Victor moved toward the sidewalk and trailed Maude. At least fifty or so people were already in line to buy tickets though the chapel wouldn't open for another ten minutes. He would be the morning guide and would give two lectures within the chapel. Before that happened, however, Victor wanted to make damn sure that he would be allowed in. Taking a deep breath, he moved forward and caught up with silver-haired Maude.

Maude was dressed in a lavender dress and was slightly hunched over. She stood by the door, the keys dangling in her arthritic fingers.

"Good morning to you, Miss Maude," Victor

said, nodding deferentially to the eighty-year-old with permed gray hair about her head.

"Morning to you, Cameron. Full schedule today, eh? We've got five busloads of people coming to the chapel today, so you're going to be busy, laddie." She put the key into the lock and turned it.

Nodding, Victor smiled. "I like busy days, Miss Maude." He stood at the door, pulled on the metal handle. The heavy timber door yawned open and revealed the beauty inside the chapel. Heart pounding, Victor took a step across the threshold. And then another. He was in the chapel. Would Sophia block him?

As he looked around at the splendor of the sculptures, the creamy-colored stone ribs that arced from floor to an apex at the ceiling, Victor was impressed. He could feel the palpable light energy throbbing out of the crypt area off to his left. Because he was in a human body, he could withstand the light energy. It would not touch him. Rather, it would be absorbed by the body he possessed. Waiting, Victor felt no resistance. The last time he'd come face-to-face with Sophia was in Petra in the country of Jordan. That red-and-pink city carved from soft sand-stone was another place she guarded for the

Taqe. There, as he'd tried to enter in spirit, he'd gotten spun backward so swiftly that his spirit remained bruised for weeks afterward.

Victor stood tensely. Sophia wasn't reacting. *Good!* He was being allowed to enter this sacred space incognito! Moving swiftly through the empty chapel, Victor went to get things ready for the first guided tour of the day. He felt the continual wash of energy that throbbed within this massive stone monument. The vortex here was huge and powerful. Moving to the left, Victor sensed that the sphere was located somewhere in the crypt.

Glee sizzled through him as he quickly made his way between the long wooden pews to the crypt. Steep yellow sandstone stairs led down to the empty room below. Standing there, Victor sensed that an emerald sphere resided somewhere down in that gloomy darkness. He saw lights, but they were not on so he walked over to the electric panel and flipped the switch. A plan formed in his mind.

Turning on his heel, he rapidly walked out of the front door and found Maude ambling slowly with her wooden cane toward the office.

"Miss Maude?" he called, hurrying to catch up with her.

"Eh?" Maude turned, squinted and then smiled. "Ah, Cameron. What is it, laddie?"

Out of breath, Victor smiled at the old woman who was barely five feet tall. Her face was broad and square. "Miss Maude?" Victor leaned close, his lips near her ear, and whispered, "I thought I saw a rat running across the crypt floor just now."

"Oh, my!" Maude said, her eyes flying wide. "Why, that's unacceptable! We've never had rats or mice in here!"

Nodding and looking worried, Victor said, "Is Ian around?" Ian was the groundskeeper and in charge of such things.

"No, he's not due until noon today," Maude said, worried. "This is not good, Cameron. We can't have a rat in our chapel! The good folk coming here would be appalled. What can we do?"

"No, ma'am, we can't. Can you stand outside the door for about ten minutes? I think I can catch it and get rid of it."

"Of course I can. I'll make up an excuse that we're not quite ready yet and the tourists will understand," Maude said, seeming relieved.

Victor could see she swallowed this without a problem. He itched to get the time to search the crypt without interference. Maude hobbled out the door and he shut it. Now, she was standing like a big guard dog out there and he had the uninterrupted minutes!

Victor chuckled to himself as he hurried down the stone steps, the echo loud. With his psychic senses turned on, Victor stood in the empty space. The crypt floor was blackened with wear and time, and the walls had turned gray. Quiet chilliness surrounded him. He felt the powerful movement of the vortex. In fact, his body swayed slightly back and forth to the rhythm of the whirling tornado-like energy. Where could the sphere be? Quickly searching, Victor noted two square niches chiseled into the north wall. They were empty. Moving quickly he saw a chamber on the north wall without a door. Peeking inside, he found several wooden shelves with various pieces of sculptured rock that had come from the chapel itself. *No sphere.* Chuckling darkly over his scheme, Victor moved to the east wall. A huge gray stone altar had been built into the wall. A Templar cross was on the front of it along with a large stained glass window depicting Jesus. *Nothing there.* Victor walked to the south wall in which four niches of various shapes and sizes had been built. And there was a door which he quickly went to and opened. Chiseled into the stone beneath the door was what looked like a bird's foot. He had no idea what that meant and pushed into the small, empty room. *No sphere.* Closing the door, he passed a fireplace and a final rectangular niche. *Nothing.* He stood at the bottom of the stairs, hands on his hips, scowling.

The crypt was not humid or musty. Instead, fresh air circulated, though the lighting was poor at best. He opened his senses and could not feel a sphere anywhere. He knew from other missions that the emerald would never reveal itself to anyone except a *Taqe* with the Vesica Pisces birthmark on his or her neck. And in this case, he was sure Mary Anderson would be able to call the sphere out of wherever it was hiding. Cursing softly, Victor realized he had to give up. He glanced down at his watch. Time for Maude to open the door to the hordes of tourists. His ten minutes were just about up. Taking the steps two at a time, he went to play tour guide.

Nicholas held Mary's hand as they stood in line to take the next lecture within Rosslyn Chapel. Today, Nicholas wore a bright-blue polo shirt, tasteful and conservative dark brown trousers and comfortable sneakers. They'd had a wonderful breakfast at the Hillwood B and B, rented a car and driven to the chapel. He felt the Dark Lord was near. Mary seemed oblivious to it, her cheeks flushed and eyes sparkling from their lovemaking. Smiling to himself, Nicholas continued to absorb the satisfied glow in his loins. He gave her fingers a squeeze, leaned over and said, "What are you sensing?"

Mary looked up at him, content at his side. "Not much. I'm still thinking of other things." She grinned. Nicholas returned her smile and heat flooded her. He squeezed her hand. "Okay," she murmured, "according to my dream, the spheres are in the crypt."

Nodding, Nicholas shuffled along with the rest of the tourists going forward to pay for their entrance tickets. The sun was snuffed out with low-hanging clouds this morning. He could smell the ocean scent on the breeze. "First we have to get in there and go to the crypt. It says on the brochure that the tour is only about the main chapel. The crypt is open but ignored."

"Maybe we'll be alone, then?" she asked. An orange butterfly winged by and Mary pulled her rust-colored nylon jacket more tightly against her. It was around fifty-five degrees and the breeze was keeping the morning chilly. Because it looked as though it might rain, Mary had pulled on a cozy pink angora sweater with a mock turtleneck along with a pair of chocolate corduroy slacks. The sweater kept her warm, but Nicholas's look made her burn inwardly.

They walked down the path and onto the grounds. Signs pointed for them to go to the chapel's west entrance. Nicholas felt a wave of energy wash over him. And it wasn't a good feeling. Shifting his gaze toward the opened door to the chapel, he saw a young Scottish lad with the words *Tour Guide* in red letters across his dark green jacket. Eyes narrowing, Nicholas examined the boy's aura. It was dirty, and the youth was pale. What was he seeing? A sick youth or was it possible the Dark Lord himself was in possession of him? Unsure, Nicholas kept the bubble of protection around Mary and himself.

Victor remained with his eyes on the crowd. *There!* He felt the *Taqe* energy as if it had slapped him in the face. And he was being watched. He could feel it. Excitement thrummed through

Victor as he stood near the door welcoming the incoming visitors. He knew not to lift his head and stare at the people shuffling into the chapel. That would be a dead giveaway to the warrior, Nicholas de Beaufort. Victor was more interested in the woman at his side, Mary Anderson. She was the key to this puzzle.

Finally, everyone gathered around Victor in the center of the magnificent chapel. He greeted them and waited for the last stragglers to enter the chapel before he began his spiel. He burned Mary's face into his memory. There was such love emanating from her that it scared the hell out of him. The friendly warmth in her blue eyes forced him to look away. One could pull the spirit out of a person's body through their eyes. Even though he was sure Mary Anderson wasn't a sorcerer like himself, Victor wasn't about to lock gazes with her, either. Now he understood why she had been chosen to find the next sphere.

Girding himself, Victor could taste the energy from the Templar knight who stood at the back of the assembled crowd. The power of de Beaufort shook him. Glad they were inside now, he took a ragged breath. Was this knight as powerful as he was? Victor was unsure and didn't try to answer the question. Everyone had limits to their power. In four thousand years, Victor had not felt a *Taqe* Warrior for the Light like this and he became edgy. Thankful that he was well-hidden in a bubble of protection, Victor wondered if the knight had powers to see through all of his walls of security.

"Did you feel that?" Mary asked Nicholas in a hushed tone. They were in back of the gathering tourists within the chapel. Everyone spoke in quiet, respectful tones because they were in a place of religious worship.

"Yes."

"Something's wrong with that guide. Did you see his eyes? They looked flat and dead."

Nicholas drew Mary back against the wall, his voice low. "That's a *Tupay*," he warned her. "And unless I miss my guess, he's possessed that poor boy."

Shivering, Mary nodded. The chapel was warm in comparison to the breeze and temperature outside. "Thanks for warning me. I wouldn't have known if you hadn't said anything."

"You're learning," Nicholas said grimly. He put his arm around Mary's shoulders. Above all, he wanted her as far away from that guide as possible.

"Will he—hurt us?" she asked, gazing up at

him. Right now, Nicholas looked like a warrior ready for battle. His mouth was tense, his eyes narrowed and she could feel the power focused to a laser intensity around him.

"No." Nicholas was fairly sure whoever had possessed the lad wasn't a low-grade field knight. On the contrary, he was smart and a top-echelon *Tupay* knight. They never attacked openly. What confounded Nicholas was that Sophia would allow a *Tupay,* even in a possessed human body, into this sacred *Taqe* space. Shaking his head, he realized that Sophia rarely interfered in a human being's karma and lessons.

Mary studied the guide as he began his enthusiastic talk to the assembled tourists. Opening herself a little, she noticed his muddy aura. But most of all, she was aware of the fact that he refused to meet her gaze as he talked to the group. Why? Either he didn't see her as anything more than an interested tourist. Or he knew exactly who she was and had other plans. Her body chilled at the thought…and the fear over what lay ahead.

Chapter 13

Nicholas kept them at the rear of the group. As Cameron, the "guide," gave a lively talk about Rosslyn Chapel, Nicholas maneuvered Mary away from the group. To the left was the crypt area and no one was down in that area right now. He cupped her shoulder and guided her over to the Apprentice Pillar, which twisted upward with beautiful sculptures. The pillar stood next to the stairs that led down into the crypt.

Mary halted. Suddenly dizzy, she leaned against Nicholas. "The power in the crypt is strong," she murmured.

"In your dream you said the spheres were in safekeeping in two different niches in the crypt's walls down there."

"It's true. I saw this crypt and I know which niches are involved." She twisted a look up at him. His face was expressionless, his eyes narrowed upon the blackened stone floor of the crypt.

"Good. Are you dizzy? The power emanating from that crypt area is affecting me."

"Yes," Mary admitted. She was glad for his arm around her shoulders. "I feel buffeted by the energy."

"There's a vortex that this crypt was built over long before the chapel was ever constructed," he told her, keeping an eye on the group. "This place goes as far back as Lemuria, when humans began to move from spirit into human form. Later, during the period of Mu, it was a sacred temple to the Great Mother Goddess. When Atlantis became the third stage of Earth's epochs, the temple was torn down and rebuilt. All of Atlantis came here to this very spot to worship the Mother one day a year. At that time it had been a healing temple and miracles happened all the time. After Atlantis sank beneath the waves, the Iron Age people discovered this area and created a circle of rocks. The

Vikings then found it and continued the circle. Druids came and then, St. Clair relatives got here. They were from Viking stock and laid the foundation you see here now and built a four-walled building."

Nicholas pointed to the stairs. "There was a wall there at one time with important ceremonial markings, but the Earl of Rosslyn, who built the chapel, had it torn down and these stairs installed, instead. That's the power force you're feeling. Ancient power from the time the Earth was young. Come on, we need to get back with the group before we arouse suspicion."

As they joined their group, Mary asked, "How do we get down there?"

"I'm going to talk to someone in the office. We have to get access to that place after the tours are finished for the day."

"What about Cameron Lindsay? If he's possessed, will he hang around here after the tourists have left?" Mary wondered.

"I don't know, but he'll be near the chapel. I doubt he can do anything to us so long as we are in here. Once we step out that door though, we're targets."

Shivering, Mary edged between the people and stared briefly at Cameron. He was enthusiastically explaining the different pillars and the cube-like stones in the thirteen arches that formed the stone ribs supporting the Mary Chapel. That same sense of danger crawled through her.

"Come on," Nicholas said, "we've got the info we needed. Let's go to the office. I have a plan."

Mary was glad to get away. Nicholas went to talk with the manager of the chapel, Robert Garnock, while Mary sat in a wing chair out front near the desk where the female assistant worked diligently on the computer. Would Nicholas be able to get access? Biting her lower lip, hands clasped in her lap, Mary felt anxious. She was relieved to escape from Cameron, but it seemed as if invisible walls were slowly moving toward her to squash her out of existence.

"We're in," Nicholas told her triumphantly as he ushered her out the door of the office. The sun was peeking through the grayish stratus clouds, the temperature rising a little more. He placed his hand in hers and led her to the parking lot.

"Wonderful," Mary said, scooting into the rental car. Nicholas closed the door. After getting in, he started the car and they drove back to the Hillwood B and B.

Nicholas noticed the stress lingering at the corners of her luscious mouth. "He's not following us," he said.

"You wiped out our energy trail?" Mary was learning so much from Nicholas. She hadn't realized that everyone had an energy trail, no matter whether they walked, flew or drove in a car. One of the ways a sorcerer could stalk a person was by following that energy trail.

"Oh, yes," Nicholas replied. He smiled into her dark blue eyes. Her black lashes were thick and long, like a beautiful frame around them. "Whoever possessed that young man won't be finding us. I've made sure of that."

More relief fled through Mary. "When do we go back?"

"This evening, near dusk."

"That was nice of the manager to let us back in."

"Yes," Nicholas replied, looking around at the rolling green hills, the glens and knots of trees. "I told him you would like to meditate in the crypt, that you were writing a book about Rosslyn. He liked the idea that you would give the chapel a fair and balanced presentation in your book. Plus a nice dedication."

Smiling, Mary said, "I'm not writing a book, Nicholas."

"That's not a lie I told him," he said, warming beneath her sparkling blue gaze. "Someday, you *will* pen a book about all of this."

"So you can see our future?"

Grimacing, Nicholas murmured, "Some, not all of it." He wished he could. Above all, he couldn't tell Mary how much danger they would be in this evening. He kept the conversation light in an effort to get her to relax, but he knew Mary could feel a threat. She was prone to being frightened easily because she had no training in how to protect herself from someone like the Dark Lord. Nicholas grudgingly admitted few could ever confront the Dark Lord and live to tell about it. Did they even stand a chance?

Victor waited impatiently. He'd talked with Garnock earlier and the man had divulged that two special "guests" were coming back at dusk. He was excited that Mary Anderson was a writer and that she would provide a fair assessment of Rosslyn Chapel. Victor was thrilled, as well, but for a different reason. He ordered four of his most powerful knights, including Lothar, to come and possess humans so they could assist him once Mary Anderson found the sphere. This time, Victor would not be denied. As he stood by the open door of the chapel greeting the last group of the day, eager to begin the guided presentation, Victor could see four of the men had been possessed.

Rubbing his hands, Victor allowed himself to feel a little giddy. By sunset, he'd have that next sphere. And instead of having only one, he would possess two.

Dusk was a dark reddish color along the western horizon. Mary wondered if it was a warning, a danger sign. As the manager, Robert Garnock, escorted them into the chapel and to the crypt stairs, she kept her thoughts to herself.

"There you go," the manager said. "Stay as long as you want. Just padlock it when you're done." He pointed toward the closed front door. "All you have to do is close the door when you leave and it will automatically lock. Questions?" He watched them with a smile.

"None. Thank you so much, Mr. Garnock. We really appreciate your help with my book project," Mary said.

"Not at all, lassie. Have a good time. My janitor will arrive at 9:00 p.m. to clean the chapel and turn off the lights. Good night."

Mary watched as the brisk, lean man left the chapel. She had not seen Cameron around but sensed he was hiding outside watching them. She turned to Nicholas. "I'm ready. Are you?"

"Never more than now," Nicholas said, his hand on the small of her back as they started down the crypt stairs. With the lights on, the basement still bore a grayish tinge.

Mary carefully moved down the steep sand-stone stairs, her heart pounding. At the bottom, she and Nicholas stood on the black stone floor.

"Go ahead," Nicholas urged. "I'm the guardian, remember?" and he grinned to disarm the tension he saw in Mary's expression.

"I hope that I can do this," she began, frowning. "I'm questioning myself. And even if the spheres do appear, what then?"

Nicholas shook his head. "I don't know, Mary. We're on our own. At some point, Alaria and Adaire will contact us. I haven't heard from them yet." He forced an expression of courage he didn't feel. "We'll be fine. Just go ahead and follow the instructions you received in your dream."

Mary watched as he remained by the stairs, his hands clasped in front of him. He was like a fierce mastiff protecting her. She moved to the north wall and the second niche she'd seen in her dream. There was a song she was to sing. Mary didn't know why and didn't understand the words. They were foreign to her. Nicholas didn't know the language, either, but it didn't matter. She had to sing this song in front of this square gray-stone niche.

First thing, Mary grounded herself. She closed her eyes and allowed the energy of the place to swell and fill her from head to toe.

Nicholas watched Mary's aura change and shift as she grounded. The energy of the vortex began to whirl faster and faster as she connected to it. Her aura glowed from silver into golden colors. That meant that Sophia, the guardian of this sacred place, was now connected directly with Mary. Sophia appeared out of the ether above the altar and drifted over to behind where Mary stood. Fascinated, he watched the guardian open her hands, her fingers touching either end at the top of the niche as Mary began to sing.

Mary's eyes remained closed and she inhaled deeply. The beautiful, unknown melody whispered from her lips. The sound of her voice was strong and moving as she sang. Though dizzy from the whirling motion, Mary kept her eyes closed. No matter what, the sphere in this tomb said to continue to sing the notes of this song over and over again until it appeared.

In her psychic third eye located in the center of her brow, Mary noticed a greenish color emanating from the back of the niche. She felt as if someone were playing a kettle drum, the vibration so powerful that the sound resonated through her. She kept her knees slightly flexed so that the grounding energy could anchor her. That was the only way to deal with energies like this. All her fear dissolved. In its place Mary began to feel not only peace but love. It filled her as if she were an empty vessel. By the time she absorbed the green energy into herself, the emanations at the center of the niche brightened.

She continued to sing the song. Opening her eyes, Mary was awed by how the entire crypt bathed in the emerald-and-gold energy. It was breathtaking. Feeling light and joyous, she witnessed the first sphere as it winked into the third dimension and hovered in the center of the niche. She stretched out her hand, palm up, still singing. The flashing gold in the depths of the golf-ball-sized orb deepened. It wafted through the air toward Mary's opened hand.

Within moments, the sphere rested in her palm. As she finished the song, Mary stared down at the glorious emerald sphere and felt its deep faith. Nicholas had told her that the last two spheres were about faith and love. This one was faith, she was sure. Turning, she saw Nicholas come forward, happiness in his eyes. He had brought over one of the two leather pouches and opened it.

"One down, one to go," she whispered as she placed the sphere gently into the bag.

"How are you doing?" he asked, closing the laces and placing it in his left hand.

"Okay," Mary said. "I feel incredibly light and happy."

"Good. Go for the second one."

"How much time elapsed?" she asked, walking to the south wall with its more ornate niche. It was square on the bottom with a beautiful bowl and sculpted flowers. The top of the niche resembled Moorish art with curves coming to a point.

"Fifteen minutes. You're doing fine, beloved."

Giving him a tender look, Mary felt the full effects of the energy—and the love she had held for Nicholas through thousands of years of lives shared with one another. Retrieving the emerald sphere had sharpened her understanding not only of their connection, but of the reasons why it was so important to string the Emerald Key Necklace back together once more.

Once again, Mary closed her eyes and began to sing. This time, it went more quickly. The last sphere, the one inscribed with *love,* appeared in the niche. She lifted her hand to receive it, relishing how this sphere was even more beautiful than the last.

As it settled into Mary's hand, she felt her heart bursting wide open. All past wounds were now healed, such was the miraculous power of this special orb. Her song ceased and she marveled at the emerald nestled in her palm. Not only did it flash gold, but all the colors of the rainbow.

Nicholas came forward with the second pouch open to receive the sphere.

"This one is special, Nicholas," Mary said.

"I can see that," he murmured. As Mary eased the second orb into the other pouch, Nicholas received the energy into his aura and physical body. He embraced the energy of this gemstone, his eyes shuttering closed. He'd not expected anything to happen, but all the wounds he carried from the time he'd been burned to death disappeared in a heartbeat. He felt the gem scouring every nook and cranny of all his thousands of lifetimes. And in what seemed seconds, the sphere washed him clean of any heavy energy. It left his body. Forever.

Opening his eyes, he stared in amazement at Mary, who was smiling up at him. "Did this happen to you, too? The cleansing of heavy energy?"

Mary nodded and took the two pouches. In the dream, she had been told to place them in her quilted shoulder bag. "Yes, the same. I feel as if I'm a newborn with nothing but innocence. Is that how you feel?"

Leaning down, he retrieved her quilted handbag. "Yes," he murmured, awe in his tone. He felt the connection between their hearts, and understood at a deep, unfathomable level that love was the only way to live. Reaching out, he caressed her rosy-red cheek. "I love you, Mary. I feel the oneness with you as never before." His voice quavered. Nicholas was unable to put into words the incredible love he held for his soul mate.

Her eyes glistened with tears, her soft lips parting. "It's as if we are nothing but pure love now, Nicholas," she whispered unsteadily, "without all the walls, the hurt, the heavy energy we carried in lifetimes before this one." Mary took the quilted handbag and placed the two spheres within it. She felt the emanations flood her like warm love flowing through her in a ripple effect, each wave a little deeper, a little wider than the last.

Stepping forward, Nicholas obeyed his heart. "You are mine," he whispered and framed her upturned face. "We are one." He leaned down and brushed her waiting lips. His mouth cherished hers, their breathing becoming one. He brought her into the circle of his arms and held her tightly against him. As he did so, the emeralds' energy enfolded and engulfed him. As their mouths clung greedily to one another, Nicholas felt something new happen. It was as if his body were moving into hers, and hers was moving into his. The sensation was warm and wonderful, but it wasn't happening in reality. As they made this transformation on the energy level, Nicholas felt whole and complete.

"Did you feel that?" he said, gazing deeply into Mary's eyes.

Mary lifted her hand and cupped his cheek. "I did. Now I understand what it means to say that you are my soul mate. We are each one half of the soul. I am the feminine part and you are the masculine." Mary felt so spaced-out by the change that she could only smile and absorb the smile he gave her in return. *One!* They were truly one. The feeling of soaring happiness, of union, was what all soul mates pined for, yearned for. Mary had no idea how often this happened. For her, it was an unexpected miracle. A blessing of the highest order. Her physical body vibrated as if she were standing on a floor that was trembling during an earthquake.

"I feel—so different," she admitted, as Nicholas released her from his embrace. Searching his green eyes, she asked, "Do you, too?"

"Very," Nicholas replied, his voice filled with awe. While scanning the poorly lit crypt, he realized that the green haze within the area had disappeared and now, it glowed from Mary's quilted shoulder bag. He touched her shoulder. "Are you feeling okay?"

Laughing a little, Mary said, "I feel spaced out. As though my feet aren't quite on the ground."

"That's because you're carrying two of those spheres," he noted wryly.

Her eyes widened. "I can't even begin to realize what Ana will feel like when she wears the necklace. She must be incredibly solid."

"We are still missing one. Alaria said they were working to get it back."

Mary looked toward the stairs. There was a

silence filled with loving energy. The chapel seemed to have adopted a golden glow within. "What do we do now? Did Alaria tell you?"

Nicholas shook his head. "No. We may have to get out of the chapel in order to contact them. In the past, they have transported the mission team directly to the Village of the Clouds."

"Why do we have to leave here?" Mary asked, not wanting to walk away from this sacred, beautiful chapel.

Nicholas shrugged. "The laws of the Great Mother Goddess state that no actions may be taken in a sacred space. That goes for us, too. We're going to have to leave and get far enough away from our bubble of protection for anything else to happen."

"I see," Mary said, the logic making sense to her. She walked up to Nicholas. "I'm ready."

"So am I." Nicholas felt a deep fear beneath all the loving energy circulating within him. He cupped her elbow to steady her as they climbed the stairs.

Mary's new confidence helped dissipate the feeling of danger. As Nicholas's hand cupped her elbow, she basked in the love flowing into her so powerfully that she ached to love him thoroughly. When this mission was over, Mary promised herself she would do just that.

At the stop of the stairs, Nicholas halted and they both stood mesmerized by the pulsing gold color everywhere within the chapel and crypt. "Look at that," he said, smiling. "Releasing these spheres has helped the vortex here to amass even more power. Amazing."

"I only wish people could see this."

"They won't," Nicholas said, leading Mary down past the pews, "but they'll feel it. They'll get a chance to absorb this newly released healing energy tomorrow morning. Lucky people."

"I hope it helps them as much as it just helped us, Nicholas."

They halted near the door, and Nicholas released her elbow. Lifting his hand, he brushed black curls away from her temple. Mary's cheeks were now pink. The energy had pumped through her body and now, her aura had adjusted to this new vibration. "I hope so, too," he murmured.

Nicholas forced himself to go on internal and external guard. When they walked through that door, they would be targets of the Dark Lord. The only question was whether Alaria and Adaire could help protect them. Nicholas didn't know. He had to prepare to stop any *Tupay* from trying to possess Mary. Even if it meant his death.

Chapter 14

"Are you ready?" Nicholas said as they hesitated at the chapel door. He could feel the intense anxiety coming from Mary. She held the quilted shoulder bag beneath her left arm, her knuckles white around the cloth strap. The two green spheres emanated light.

"I am," she said, shooting a look at him. His face was deeply shaded, making him look both handsome and dangerous. But as menacing as he might be for an enemy, she could feel his intense protectiveness. His eyes were fixed on what lay beyond the thick dark door. What awaited them out there? Surely Victor Guerra, the Dark Lord, would be nearby. He wasn't stupid and he wanted the spheres. "Do you think Guerra realizes we have two spheres?"

Nicholas slid his hand around her shoulders and gave her a gentle squeeze. "I don't think so." His mouth thinned. "If he does, he'll become even more aggressive." Nicholas worried about a lot of things and this wasn't one of them. The Great Mother Goddess had allowed them to retrieve the spheres in this sacred place, and he had a hunch that Guerra himself had been the guide, Cameron, earlier today. She had allowed the *Tupay* into this hallowed place. That told Nicholas that all bets were off; the Goddess would let this play out on a human level, and she would not interfere. That's the way it always was when humans were at a point of either making or breaking a step forward in their evolution. It was up to them. And in reality, it fell heavily upon his shoulders. Inhaling slowly, Nicholas visualized a heavy bubble of protection around them. Would it be enough to stop a direct assault by the Dark Lord and his minions?

Victor waited, tension thrumming through him. He had brought his most powerful *Tupay* knights. They stood just beyond the chapel's bubble of protection. He wouldn't be allowed to attack Mary Anderson and the Templar knight-monk guard dog within the sacred bounds of the chapel. If they tried, they would all be instantly fried, their souls destroyed and gone forever, without recourse.

Instead, in the late evening, the sky a deep purple with a black coverlet above it, he and his men waited in a small grove of trees near the curb of the road. Anxiety rifled through Victor. What if Nicholas and Mary stepped out of the chapel and were instantly dematerialized to the Village of the Clouds with the latest sphere? His hand flexed into a fist—Victor didn't like that thought. And yet, other times when the mission specialists for the *Taqe* had found the emerald spheres, they instantly went to the safety of the *Taqe* stronghold.

"My lord!" Lothar croaked, his eyes wide with shock. "I just received a message from your office. The emerald sphere is *gone!*"

A collective gasp exploded from the awaiting group.

Whirling around, Victor snarled, "What are you talking about?" No one could steal his emerald! No one!

Lothar's face worked with the shocking news.

His knight had been instructed to take all incoming messages, leaving Victor free to focus on stealing the emerald once the *Taqe* emerged from the chapel.

"My lord, your office assistant just said that the safe in your office was open when he went in to put some information on your desk," stuttered Lothar. "He said the safe was opened and the sphere is gone!"

Victor cursed roundly, glaring at Lothar. "Who could steal it, you simpleton?"

"I don't know, my lord," Lothar murmured. "What *Tupay* in his right mind would steal it from you?"

Victor glared at Lothar and then turned back to the chapel. The *Taqe* were still inside, but had they found the sphere yet? He had to divide and conquer. His first priority had now changed. Victor poked Lothar in the chest with his index finger. "You are in charge of getting that emerald from those two. Don't screw up on this, Lothar. I'll be back as soon as I can."

Lothar watched the Dark Lord exit Cameron Lindsay's body like dark smoke shooting out of the top of the lad's head and then disappearing into the fourth dimension. The body crumpled at Lothar's feet. He hitched a thumb toward the grove. "Take his body out of here. Dump it somewhere unseen. Now!"

Lothar watched as two knights picked up Cameron, now dead, and quickly hustled him off through the grove. Turning, Lothar scowled. Now he was worried. The Dark Lord was the most powerful sorcerer in the universe. Without him here, he questioned whether he and his *Tupay* knights were strong enough to overwhelm the Templar knight-monk with the woman. Terror sizzled through him. He didn't want to disappoint the Dark Lord.

Even as he set to his new task, he couldn't stop wondering who had stolen the emerald. Whoever it was, the Dark Lord himself would kill him. Who was stupid enough to defy Victor Guerra? Wiping his mouth, Lothar glanced up at the darkening sky above. Some *Tupay* had turned traitor. That or they had desired power and stolen it. Either way, that soul was a dead spirit walking….

Jeff's heart pounded in his chest as he stood uncertainly at the foot of the small wooden bridge. He heard the water burbling merrily, but he felt nothing but fear mixing violently with anxiety. In his hand was the pouch that contained the emerald sphere he'd stolen from the Dark Lord's office.

He looked around, noticing how he was surrounded by a white, fog-like mist. Alaria, the elder woman leader from the *Taqe* Village of the Clouds, had said she'd meet him at the bridge once he'd stolen the sphere and brought it here. He shifted nervously from foot to foot. Most of all, he wanted to protect his granddaughter, Mary Anderson. Was she safe? Jeff had watched her enter the chapel, unbeknownst to Victor Guerra and his assembled knights who waited outside to apprehend them. It was then that Jeff had sneaked into Guerra's office and opened the safe.

Where was Alaria? Would she appear? Jeff turned around and kept looking for her. Soon, the mist completely enclosed him and he could no longer see. No sounds. Just peaceful quiet. Gripping the pouch in his right hand, he glanced toward the bridge.

"Greetings, my son," Alaria said, materializing at the center of the bridge.

"Ah," Jeff whispered, suddenly relieved. "You came…."

Alaria smiled. "A promise is a promise. You have the emerald sphere?"

He nodded. "I do. But I'm worried, Grand-mother."

"About?"

"My granddaughter." He frowned. "You said you couldn't interfere if they attacked her."

Giving him a sad look, Alaria said, "The Great Mother Goddess has decreed that we cannot interfere to help Mary or Nicholas. I'm sorry. We are hoping that your courageous act will draw the Dark Lord out of the fray we know will occur. That alone will make the confronta-tion more equal."

"He's got six of his most powerful *Tupay* knights down there waiting for Mary to walk out of that chapel!" Jeff cried, his voice rising in alarm. "I don't call that equal, do you?"

Alaria eyed him with compassion. "My son, nothing in any world or dimension is ever easy or straightforward. Nicholas de Beaufort is our most powerful *Taqe* knight. We have done every-thing we can to tip the balance in Mary's favor."

Tears came to Jeff's eyes. The warmth and love emanating from Alaria was food for his starving, anxiety-ridden soul. He began to real-ize how barren of positive human emotions the *Tupay* castle had been. "Grandmother, I have a question to ask you. A technical one."

"Of course," Alaria said, folding her hands within the sleeves of her peach-colored robe.

"If I cross this bridge, I turn from *Tupay* to *Taqe?*"

"That is correct."

"But if I don't cross it, I remain *Tupay?*"

Frowning, Alaria said, "Yes, that is so. Why do you ask? I thought you wanted to become *Taqe* like your granddaughter."

Jeff rubbed his furrowed brow. "I need to go down there to try and help Mary. I can't let her be possessed and killed. I can try to help her and Nicholas."

"My son, please, do not do this."

"Don't worry," Jeff said, holding up the leather pouch toward her. "I'll give you the sphere. I just don't feel there's enough protection for Mary."

"But," Alaria said, alarm in her husky tone, "if you go down there and the Dark Lord knows you're the one who stole the emerald, he will kill you."

Jeff shrugged. "I come from a time when patriotism, loyalty and duty to one's country and family were important, Grandmother. Right now, the most important thing to me is my beautiful granddaughter. I would gladly give up my life so that she can live. Here…I'm going to toss you the pouch. If our fingers touch, I will turn into *Taqe,* and I can't do that. Not yet. Are you ready to catch the pouch?"

"Yes, give it to me, Jeff," Alaria said, opening her hands.

With a gentle toss, Jeff released the pouch. It flew through the air and landed safely in Alaria's cupped hands. Satisfaction moved through him. "Good. Now you have all the emeralds. I need to go, Grandmother. Can you get me out of this fog and send me to Mary?" He gave her a pleading look.

"Of course, my son. But realize you have our blessing and prayers. What you've done will help move Earth toward the light if Mary and Nicholas can bring the last two spheres of the Emerald Key Necklace to us."

Jeff felt anxious. "Thanks. I appreciate your help in getting me to my granddaughter."

"Are you ready?" Nicholas asked Mary. He'd just received a telepathic transmission from Alaria that the emerald Jeff had stolen from the Dark Lord was safely with Alaria. Now they had to face the wrath of the heavy-energy forces.

"As ready as I'll ever be," Mary said, her hand tight on her shoulder bag.

"Good. The car I rented is in the parking lot, about five hundred feet away." Nicholas had no idea what had to be done to get the spheres to the Village of the Clouds. They were on their own and Nicholas didn't know for how long.

Mary turned toward him, her right hand resting upon his dark brown leather jacket. "I love you, Nicholas. No matter what happens, just know that."

Looking deeply into her wide blue eyes, Nicholas leaned down and brushed her parted lips. "Beloved, we carry a love that cannot ever be destroyed. Not by them, nor by anything else. Hold on to that and have faith." He smiled and brushed his fingers across the soft curls at her temple.

Mary felt his love enter her, interrupting the storm of fear that churned within her. His love flowed through her and dissolved her anxiety and fear of dying. She drowned in his gleaming eyes that clearly showed him for the courageous warrior he was. "I'll try. I have to believe in this love. It has transcended time, after all."

"That is what you must cling to, beloved." He squeezed her shoulder. "You have the keys to the car. You know our plan. If we have to split up, you're to drive to the chapel and if you see me, pick me up. And if I don't show, you are to drive toward Glastonbury in southwest England. The Chalice Wells is another *Taqe* sacred area and there you will be safe from any attacks. That is your next destination."

It was a good plan and Mary nodded. "Okay, let's go…."

Nicholas swung open the door. The street lamps were on, casting conical areas of light across the lawn in front of the chapel. He sent a prayer to the Great Mother Goddess and then quickly brought Mary along, her hand in his. All his awareness and focus was on the waiting *Tupay*.

The dusk air had a chill to it, the humidity was high and the scent of the ocean was upon the air. Nicholas's hand was tight around Mary's as she nearly ran to keep up with his long strides across the lawn toward the only exit. The light was spotty. Outside the entrance and down a narrow, curvy asphalt path lay Chapel Close. The parking lot stood down the hill and to the left of the chapel grounds. A grove of oak, beech and chestnut trees sat off the path they trod. Mary couldn't help feeling afraid. "Nicholas…" she began.

Nicholas anchored as four men, all possessed, came out of the grove to the left of the path.

They were like ghosts congealing fifty feet below them. Instantly, he drew Mary behind him.

"Run, Mary!" he snarled. Turning, Nicholas faced the four men rushing him.

Mary wheeled around and ran toward the glen below the chapel. There was a dirt road at the bottom of the steep hill and would lead to the parking lot. The four men charging Nicholas had tree limbs in their hands.

Mary raced into the glen. Below the hill she could see street lamps showing the parking-lot area. *Hurry!* Breath ripped from her mouth as she tore down the thick, grassy slope to the brush below. There was a fence and she quickly moved through it and to the road. Nicholas! He could be killed! Mary knew his orders. She could not go back. She could not stand to protect him. She had to get to the car.

Nicholas braced himself. He saw the limbs of trees in the hands of the four men, possessed by *Tupay* knights, no doubt. Whirling on his heel, he dove down the narrow path between the wall around the chapel and a thick grove of trees toward the glen. As he exploded into the glen, he noticed Mary was gone. *Good!* He dug his heels into the soft grass and forged across the slope and down to the left of the hill. He was leading the *Tupay* in the opposite direction of the parking lot. That way, Mary could escape.

His plan worked! The *Tupay* crashed down the path and out into glen after him. Their steps were swift and he heard them gaining upon him. His eyes adjusted to the poor light, but the *Tupay* knights weren't so lucky. Human sight was far more limited, which gave Nicholas another advantage. Down below him stood a grove of trees and brush on a steep, canyon-like V that wound through the valley.

The grass was already damp with gathering dew. Nicholas slipped and stumbled but caught himself as he slipped on his seat to the bottom of the hill. He lunged past the treeline and quickly dove into the darkest part. There were thickets everywhere in which to hide. Leaning down, Nicholas scooped up a broken oak limb about five feet long. It was as long as the sword he'd carried as a Templar. He skidded to a halt, breathing hard, and waited, hands around the limb. Tonight, this would be his sword of justice.

Hearing the huffing, the curses and stampede of footfalls coming in his direction, Nicholas could see the *Tupay* were badly disorganized. They were stumbling and falling. Some hit bushes they couldn't see because the darkness hid the obstacles. Nicholas grinned savagely, moving like a silent warrior. The nearest knight had possessed a red-haired man of thirty. Without hesitation, Nicholas raised the limb and brought it down across his head. The crack of his skull resounded thickly within the grove. The man fell, dead. The dark, churning spirit of the *Tupay* knight exited the falling body.

"Die," Nicholas rasped, pointing his finger at the hovering spirit. Energy erupted from the end of his index finger. The blazing golden energy shot toward the knight. Before he could get away, the loving light completely enveloped the knight. The *Tupay* screamed once, his cry cut off. He suddenly disappeared into the ether.

"One down," Nicholas breathed, turning on his heel toward the other three. He knew by sense alone that the Dark Lord was not among them. The odds were even now and he relished the coming fight. Skimming the ground, Nicholas felt a glimmer of hope. The Dark Lord was gone. Hunting for his precious emerald at the castle. That gave Nicholas the edge he desperately needed.

Another knight had tripped over a tree root. He went flying and landed with an "oomph!" on his stomach. Nicholas reached him and brought down the limb with lethal accuracy. He aimed for the head, the only sure way to kill an opponent. There was a cry, and then the knight exited the dead human. Automatically, Nicholas sent loving energy around the spirit, and it, too, disappeared—forever.

From behind him, Nicholas heard someone approaching. Too late! A limb crashed down, intended for his head. At the last second, with a warrior's reflexes, Nicholas turned just enough. The limb landed on his right shoulder. Uttering a cry of pain, Nicholas was driven to his knees, his weapon falling out of his right hand.

"*Taqe* dog!" Lothar snarled, leaning down to grip the Templar knight. "You're going to die. Right now…" He lifted the limb to finish off the knight.

Twisting, Nicholas reared back, his legs arcing upward. His feet slammed into the man who gripped his leather jacket. He saw the dead eyes of the man as Nicholas managed to kick at his arm, the limb coming down toward his head.

Lothar grunted as the knight's foot slammed into his chest. In an instant, he was flying backward. Surprised by the *Taqe*'s move, Lothar's hatred of this man increased tenfold.

He landed in a thicket. Flailing around, cursing, he leaped out of the bushes. Too late! Lothar looked up just in time to see the Templar's long limb aimed directly at his head. With a cry of surprise, Lothar tried to leap back, but the wall of thick bushes trapped him. In seconds, his head exploded. *Out!* He had to escape!

Before Nicholas could raise his finger to destroy the knight, the spirit blipped out of the third dimension and disappeared. Hearing his last attacker charging, Nicholas turned. The last knight was in the body of a middle-aged blond-haired man. He had his limb held up over his head, running toward Nicholas as fast as he could.

Nicholas whirled on his feet and as the limb came down, he parried the blow by bringing his own limb above his head. They crashed together. Nicholas was thrown backward by the confrontation. The *Tupay* knight uttered a scream and fell into the thicket.

Leaping to his feet first, Nicholas witnessed his quarry flailing in the brush and trying to get up. With savage satisfaction, he swung the limb. Instantly, the man's skull cracked. Nicholas pointed at the dark cloud escaping the human's head. Within seconds, the golden light enveloped the spirit and it was destroyed—for eternity.

Breathing hard, Nicholas felt the pain radiating outward from his injured shoulder. He touched his ripped jacket where the knight's limb had landed and looked around, his breath tearing explosively out of his mouth. He knew the knight who had escaped him would warn the Dark Lord. Any moment now, Victor Guerra would be barreling back into this dimension. Nicholas dug his toes into the soil, running as fast as he could. Emerging from the grove, the night surrounding him, he rushed up the slope and galloped across the dew-laden glen. As he plunged onto the narrow path that led to Chapel Close, Nicholas saw Rosslyn swathed in lamplight, the gray stones gleaming in unearthly whites and golds.

Mary! He sent out a telepathic contact to her. She had just arrived at the car and was climbing into it. They had agreed that if they split up, she was to drive back to the chapel and, if she saw him, pick him up. Running down the narrow path, Nicholas noticed the twin beams of light stabbing into the darkness. Mary was coming for him. Wary, Nicholas slowed his pace. The Dark Lord would come. There was no question of it. But where and when would he attack? It would be, Nicholas knew, a final confrontation between light and heavy energy. Who would be victorious?

Chapter 15

"Damn them to hell!" Victor screamed. He looked disbelievingly at the opened safe. His assistant was sobbing, not because of the lost emerald—he feared for his life because Victor was furious. Whirling around, Victor glared at his assistant.

"Tell me!" he snarled, his fists balling up. How badly Victor wanted to strike out at someone. Who was the thief? It was embarrassing that he, the Dark Lord, could be stolen from so easily. Victor realized his mistake: he'd become too arrogant and sure of his power over the billions of *Tupay* who lived on Earth and lodged here at the castle to do his bidding. He'd made a strategic mistake in not understanding that not all *Tupay* were properly fearful of him or of what he could do to them. His rage boiled through him until he felt the acid burning in the back of his throat.

Just as the trembling assistant began to offer a lame excuse, Lothar appeared, angry and savage-looking.

"My lord, come immediately!"

Victor glared over at his knight. "Now what's wrong?" he snarled.

"That Templar has killed three knights. He's sent a bolt of energy that has destroyed the souls of three of them." Lothar's voice shook. "This *Taqe* is powerful. You're the only one who can fight him."

Victor cursed richly. "Can't any of you do anything right?" Shaking his finger at the assistant, he ordered, "Get a team of energy detectives on this! The bastard that stole this emerald has an energy trail. *Find it!* And before I get back or I'll destroy all of you!"

The assistant cried out, paled and fell to his knees, his hands opened in a pleading gesture. "Oh, my lord, I'm so sorry. Yes, yes, I'll get the team on it right away! I'm so sorry..."

"Shut up!" Victor yelled. Whirling around, he pinned Lothar with a glare. "Follow me!" And he disappeared.

Nicholas had just scrambled up the hill when a sudden thunderstorm struck. The lightning danced close to the chapel, the wind rising and falling with a moan. The thunder rolled across the hill and the whole area vibrated with tremors. He ran across the glen, slipping and sliding, the wind tearing at his clothes. His shoulder ached like fire itself. Nicholas realized he'd suffered some physical damage. Looking to the right, he saw car headlights coming, slowly moving toward the chapel.

Lightning struck in the grove of trees where he'd killed the *Tupay*. Nicholas turned, wondering if the Great Mother Goddess had sent the spirit of storms, known as Thunder Beings, to come and clean up the violent energy so close to the sacred chapel. Lightning danced like lace between churning dark clouds as Nicholas tried to catch his breath. *Hurry! Hurry!* he telepathed to Mary.

The car sped up toward the chapel. Nicholas braced against a blast of wind. He turned away, his back toward the grove where the *Tupay* had been hiding. His own energy was low because he'd used so much of it in the fight.

Mary watched huge splats of rain dive-bomb the windshield just as she braked and swung the car to the curb where Nicholas stood. A huge red hole whirled in the clouds near the grove in the glen. What was she seeing? She braked to a stop. Nicholas's glistening face was grim and only the flare of a nearby lightning bolt allowed her to see his fierce appearance.

The red hole in the clouds grew darker, looking like blood leaking through the clouds. Nicholas turned and looked up at it. What was it? Hands gripping the wheel, she put the car in Park near the entrance path to the chapel. Just as she climbed out, the wind gusted at over sixty miles an hour. The door was nearly ripped out of her hand. The red, lurid circle of clouds changed to look like a shark's jaws opening.

Mary screamed as a man all in black, with dead-looking eyes and a goatee, emerged from that hole. Nicholas was now racing to where the sorcerer stood in the glen. Terror sizzled through Mary. Intuitively, she knew it was the Dark Lord himself. Behind him, another man materialized, a silver sword gleaming in his hands. Her gaze tore to Nicholas. He flew toward them, his right hand held out, finger pointed at Victor Guerra.

Victor laughed at the charging *Taqe* knight. There was such focus in Nicholas's face, but it didn't scare the sorcerer. "Die, you dog," he roared, and lifted his finger. Instantly, a bolt of red lightning shot out of Victor's finger and slammed into the charging *Taqe* warrior.

Nicholas countered with golden light shooting out of his finger. It met and slammed into the garish bolt of red energy. A wild explosion lit up the night, and for a moment, Nicholas was blinded. The blast sent him sprawling on the slope of the hill. He knew the sorcerer was very close to the protective bubble of energy that enfolded and protected Rosslyn. Getting to his knees, the rain splattering around him, Nicholas saw Victor grinning savagely. The last trigger of energy had dangerously depleted Nicholas. He understood that the Dark Lord knew his advantage and would kill Nicholas.

Jerking his head to the left, he saw Mary running toward him, her face filled with fear. On her shoulder was the bag that held the spheres.

"Go back!" Nicholas roared above the thunder and the gusting wind. "Go back!"

"You're dead!" Victor shrieked at the knight

as the thunder subsided. He flew a few feet off the ground, his expression triumphant. Even better, he noted the green glow in the bag carried by the woman who thought she could save the bastard. *Good!* He had them where he wanted them. Lifting his finger, Victor willed a bolt of killing red energy once more toward the knight who was on his knees.

The red bolt zig-zagged toward the *Taqe* warrior. Victor wanted him dead. When the knight lifted his finger, golden energy blazing from it, Victor cursed.

The bolts met. An explosion of electricity blazed into the sky. The sizzle of sulfur burned the air. Victor couldn't believe it. *How strong is this bastard?* Lips pulling away from his teeth, Victor screamed at the roaring thunderstorm that swirled around them. The angry wind blasted him, forcing him to take several steps to the left to remain upright. Lothar came forward.

"Kill the girl! She's got the sphere!" Guerra yelled.

Lothar nodded and took off at a run, his sword held high above his head, aimed for Mary Anderson, who had almost reached the kneeling *Taqe* warrior.

"Mary, get out of here!" Nicholas screamed

as she slid to a stop, breathing raggedly. "I cannot hold this energy attack! Get out of here! Run to the car. Escape!"

Even as she saw the man with the sword running full tilt toward them, Mary didn't budge. "No!" she screamed above the carom of thunder. "I won't leave you! I love you!" she sobbed.

Nicholas felt his energy slowly ebbing away. Within the next few moments he would not be able to stop the deadly red energy from striking and killing his soul. Destroying him forever. *"Leave!"* he cried out to her and jerked his hand up to shove her backward.

Mary fell to the wet grass, shocked. As the man with the sword changed course from her to Nicholas, the beams of red and yellow energy met, sizzled and popped angrily. The yellow energy began to retreat.

Rain pummeled the windswept hill. Gusts tore at her as she got to her feet. Mary had no idea how to help Nicholas. The love she had for him rose up through her. Jerking the quilted bag off her shoulder, she decided that the only thing she could do was to throw one of the emerald spheres at the attacking *Tupay* knight. Maybe it would hit him and stop him. She didn't know, but she had to do something!

Grabbing one of the spheres from the bag, Mary hurled it with all her strength toward the attacking man with the sword. He was only six feet away when she threw it at him. Surprise appeared on his face. The green sphere struck the man directly in the head.

An epic explosion rocked the meadow. Mary cried with surprise as she threw up her hands to protect her eyes. The green-and-gold light flashed lightning around the entire glen. And then, she opened her eyes and blinked through the pelting rain. The man with the sword had disappeared! Confused, she saw the sphere rolling to a stop in the wet grass halfway between the angry sorcerer and Nicholas.

Victor yelped with triumph. There was the sphere! He increased his power to maximum to finish off the damned Templar knight. The man was on his knees, his left hand holding his right elbow to try and maintain the energy against him. Smiling, Victor began to walk toward the knight. His own knight, Lothar, had been killed by the thrown sphere. Well, too bad. Lothar had given his life for Victor. That's what *Tupay* knights did—died willingly for their master. This Templar knight would also die willingly.

With a snarl, Victor halted ten feet away from the knight. Clearly, the Warrior for the Light was weakening. In another three inches, the red light would reach him and he would disappear in a poof of energy, gone forever. It was then that Victor eyed the sphere glowing between them. The sphere would be his!

Mary sobbed. She held up her hand against her eyes to protect them as rain slashed wickedly through the area. Wind howled, the trees bending in the blackness. What else could she do? She saw the look of gleeful murder in Victor Guerra's pale face. His mouth was wide with a twisted smile. His hand was steady as he willed the red stream toward the man she loved.

Without thinking, she grabbed the second sphere out of her soaked bag and hurled it at the sorcerer.

Victor had a split second to react. A second sphere? There were two here at Rosslyn? He hesitated—enough that his red energy moved and allowed the gold energy to strike him. The second emerald sphere demolished Victor's spirit. Between the two assaults, his whole form began to disintegrate. *Too late!* Screaming as the energy of love funneled through every energy cell in his form, Victor convulsed.

Nicholas gasped and managed to get to his feet. The second sphere had struck the sorcerer in the heart! Nicholas turned and saw Mary standing there, her face filled with anxiety. How brave she had been! He watched as the sphere's green energy ate up the spirit of the red and black energy that had been Victor Carancho Guerra. In seconds, he disappeared. Forever.

The storm suddenly stopped. The wind became a breeze, and the lightning ceased. The rain fell to a soft patter in the glen. Feeling weak beyond anything he could ever recall, Nicholas walked unsteadily toward Mary. She turned, her eyes filled with tears, her face wet from the rain, her dark hair clinging to her skull. She cried out his name and ran into his opening arms.

When they met, Nicholas felt a surge of life directly into his pounding heart. He'd come so close to dying! As he embraced Mary, her womanly strength surrounded him and he gave a ragged sigh of relief. Closing his eyes, his head resting against her damp curls, Nicholas whispered, "I love you, Mary. I love you…."

Mary heard his whispered words, the trembling in Nicholas's deep voice. Weakened, he sagged against her. Was he dying? She wasn't sure. She braced herself so that he wouldn't fall.

And then, gold-and-white light began to fill the area. Blinking, Mary felt Nicholas steady himself. They both looked toward the glen where the life-and-death battle had just taken place. A very old woman and a tall, bearded man stood within a blinding light shaft. She heard Nicholas give an exclamation of relief. Mary recognized Alaria, with whom she'd spoken in her dream. Grinning, Adaire walked over and retrieved both spheres from the wet grass. Alaria walked toward them, beaming, her smile filling Mary with renewed hope.

"Come, my children. You have fought the darkest of the dark and won tonight." Alaria held out her hands. She placed one on a shoulder of each of them. "Close your eyes. You are going home—with us."

Mary woke slowly. Where was she? Her eyes opened to see the thatched roof above her head. As she moved her fingers outward, she felt soft woven blankets beneath her and on top of her. The pillow was soft and a scent of almonds permeated the air. She sat up, realizing she was still in her clothes. Sounds caught her groggy attention.

She heard the laughter of children and the pleasant chatter of people nearby. A bark of a dog. Songs of birds she didn't recognize. She lay on a pallet placed upon hard-packed earth. The room was simple with a curtain of pink cloth for a door. Soon, everything came back to her. Nicholas! How was he? Where was he? Anxiety began to pump through her.

She quickly threw off the covers and got to her feet. She grabbed a pair of leather sandals near the door and slipped them on. After brushing the curls away from her brow, she moved out into a large main room.

"Good morning," Nicholas greeted. He sat at the table with a mug of mint tea and a steaming bowl of oatmeal before him.

"Nicholas!" Mary was flooded with relief at the sight. He was wearing a white tunic and dark brown pants that grazed his ankles. He wore a pair of sandals like hers.

In three steps, he was at her side. "Beloved," he murmured, enfolding her in his embrace. "I'm all right and so are you," he whispered against her temple. When Mary lifted her face and their lips met, Nicholas gave a low groan of pleasure. Mary's mouth was hungry and searching. He kissed her deeply and gently ran his hand down her strong back. How brave she'd been last night! Mary had saved his life. Even more love than he could ever have fathomed existed moved through him as she clung to his searching mouth.

Mary eased her lips away and stared up at him. "Nicholas. You're all right? You really are?"

Laughing gently, Nicholas held her and rocked her in his arms. "Beloved, I am fine. And so are you. We've been brought here to the Village of the Clouds. We're safe." There was new life in her widening blue eyes along with utter relief over his whispered words. Her mouth was so soft and Nicholas ached simply to take her to bed, but she needed to be brought up to speed on the activities.

"Safe," Mary whispered. Nicholas gave her a very male smile. His green eyes were clear and she could feel the love radiating around them. "We're really safe?"

"Completely," he promised. Releasing Mary, he led her to the table. "Come, you must be hungry. As we eat, I'll fill you in on what is happening."

Mary found herself starving. Nicholas gave her half of the steaming cereal. He poured her juice made from fresh mangos that grew at the edge of the village. A bowl of brown sugar sat between them. The table was square and their knees almost touched beneath it. As she ate, Nicholas filled her in on all the activities.

"When we came here to the village last night, you were unconscious. I carried you here to our hut. Alaria said I wasn't to worry—your body had absorbed so much of the emerald spheres' energy that you were knocked senseless. She reassured me that when you woke this morning, you'd be fine." He reached over and touched her arm for a moment. "And here you are."

"What about you, Nicholas? I was so worried. I saw Guerra and the horrible look on his face. He would have been happy to kill you."

"I know," Nicholas soothed gently. "But he's no more—thanks to you. I don't know what made you throw those spheres at his knight and then at him, but it worked. Like magic."

Eating the hot, sweet cereal, Mary shrugged. She wiped her mouth on a pink napkin and placed it back across her lap. "I wanted to protect you, Nicholas. I was hoping to strike them to make them stop hurting you."

Nicholas chuckled and resumed eating. "I didn't understand what happened, either. Adaire told me later that a sphere, when thrown at someone, will change them one way or another. Neither Lothar, the knight, nor Victor realized that your grandfather, Jeff Anderson, was there and protected both of us."

"My grandfather?" Mary whispered. She set the spoon aside. "I didn't see him!"

"Nor did I," Nicholas said. He gave Mary a warm look. "Your grandfather was still a *Tupay,* so he could enter the fray without Victor or Lothar even feeling his presence. Both were too focused on you and me to see him. When you threw the sphere at Lothar, he directed it to the man's head. And when you threw the second one, the sphere with *love* written on it, it was your grandfather who carried it into the heart of Victor Guerra. The moment that sphere struck Guerra in the heart, he was a dead man."

Her eyes rounded. "My grandfather? What happened to him? Is he all right?"

Hearing the concern in her voice, Nicholas reached out and held her hand. "Jeff Anderson's act of love and protection is what saved his life after he'd carried the emerald into the heart of Guerra. Adaire found him unconscious in the fourth dimension and brought him here, to the Pool of Life. It will heal and revive him." Nicholas smiled. "Your grandfather is now a *Taqe.* Fully recovered. If not for his valor in taking the emerald sphere from Guerra's safe, we would not be ready to perform the Emerald Key ceremony. You come from a long line of warriors, Mary. And in the heat of the battle, you did what you could to protect us. I'm proud of you, beloved."

His hand anchored her and Mary closed her eyes for a moment, absorbing all the information. After a moment, she squeezed his fingers and opened her eyes. "Where is my grandfather? I would love to meet and thank him for saving us."

"In time," Nicholas counseled. "He will be at the ceremony with us."

"When Ana wears the necklace?"

"Tonight at dusk, as the sun sets, the ceremony begins. We will all assemble at the edge of the village. There we will witness a new age for the Earth, Mary."

"Thanks to you," she murmured, meaning it. Her mouth still tingled in memory of his strong lips upon hers. "All I want is to live in peace. Is that possible?"

Nicholas's brows arched for a moment. "Let's wait until the end of the ceremony. I'm sure much more will be revealed to you then, beloved."

Chapter 16

The sun was setting, the jungle sky a brilliant pink and gold. Mary stood with over three hundred people within two large circles. The formation reminded her of the wedding-ring design in quilting. Nicholas told her the two interlocked circles were known as the Vesica Pisces and had been created for the coming ceremony. She admired the white rocks that created one huge circle. The other was created out of red rocks. Nicholas told her white symbolized the male energy and red stood for the feminine principle. Combined, they created a fishlike center known as the "eye."

Mary looked around the plain, seeing people of all races, ages and color. Every religion on Earth was represented. She smiled to herself and hoped that the warmth and peace from this village would filter down to Earth. There was no need for wars or other dissension. Here, at the Village of the Clouds, she could breathe in the love of the Great Mother Goddess. The feeling was palpable, the sense of compassionate love descending upon the village. Everyone reacted to it in the same way, with gentleness, respect and smiles. There was much to smile about, Mary decided. She was lucky to be here for this very special *Taqe* event.

"Mary?"

The male voice behind her made her turn. "Yes?"

"I'm your grandfather, Jeff Anderson."

Mary gasped. Wearing a simple white shirt and blue trousers, the man was in his early twenties, his eyes bright with tears, his arms open toward her. She instantly moved into his embrace. Her heart opened and she cried. And so did Jeff. They held each other for a long time. Finally, Mary broke away from him.

"We owe our lives to you," she whispered, her voice tremulous.

Jeff nodded. "I'm glad I could help, Mary.

At first, I had problems with my role in all of this. Grandmother Alaria helped me understand that all *Tupay* are in search of the light whether they know it or not. But those who have the courage take that final step forward." He grinned shyly. "I have no regrets about what I did to help you and Nicholas." Jeff saw the Templar knight smile and thrust his hand out to the warrior.

Nicholas gripped the man's hand. "We owe you everything. If not for your courage, Jeff, we wouldn't be here."

Flushing, Jeff released his hand and grinned. "I did it because I loved my family, Nicholas. Even though I'm no longer in body, I followed my family's journey. When I found out that Mary had been chosen to find two spheres, I knew she could be killed by the Dark Lord."

"Who is gone and will never return to bother us again," Nicholas growled. "His soul has been destroyed. He'll never be able to come back."

Jeff shrugged. "Grandfather Adaire said someone else would replace him as leader of the *Tupay*."

"I'm sure someone will," Nicholas replied. He touched Mary's shoulder. She was wiping the last of the tears from her cheeks. "This is truly a happy day," he told Mary. "Now, you have your grandfather with you."

Mary reached out and drew Jeff to her side. "Stay with us. Let's watch the ceremony together."

"I'd like that," Jeff whispered, squeezing her hand and releasing it. "I wasn't sure you'd be glad to see me, Mary. I was afraid…"

"Oh, Grandfather, I could never be unhappy to see you! My mother told me many times about your heroic efforts in the war." Mary touched his arm. "I was raised knowing you were a hero. Now, I know just how heroic you really are."

Warmth penetrated Jeff's heart. He had feared she wouldn't accept him. After all, he'd been *Tupay*. And she was from the *Taqe* branch of the family. He finally felt at peace, and a sense of family unity filled his heart.

Nicholas placed his arm around Mary and she leaned against him, her head resting against his shoulder. Music came from a section of the crowd: drums, flutes and harps began to play. The music wafted up and seemed to vibrate softly in the background. Next to the instrument section was a choir of about fifty people. The elderly Scotsman who was the director stood out in front of them.

Alaria walked up with Ana, the estranged daughter of Victor Guerra. Adaire followed them. Ana was heavily pregnant. Nicholas had heard Mace, her husband, say that within two weeks their child would be born. On a white pillow in Adaire's hands lay the assembled Emerald Key Necklace. The flashing green-and-gold light was intense, shooting out rays of sunlight in all directions, bathing the huge area with its colors. As the energy throbbed around the area, Nicholas felt the vibration shift.

Mary was all eyes. She stood outside the red-and-white rock circle and had a full view of the ceremony. The music and voices in a language she did not recognize rose softly. It wasn't Latin—whatever it was, it made her heart fly open and she felt love pouring through her. Judging from the expressions on the faces of the people who encircled the Vesica Pisces symbol, they were equally touched.

Ana Ridfort had long, beautiful black hair. A circlet of purple orchids made a beautiful crown for her head. She wore a simple white cotton gown that barely touched her ankles. Around her waist was a loose, woven cotton belt that contained the colors of the rainbow. Mary was taken by the beatific expression on Ana's face.

This woman possessed the heart and love needed to wear the necklace successfully.

Nicholas leaned over and whispered to her, "Once the three of them move into the eye where the circles overlap, it will trigger powerful events. Be prepared."

She looked up at him. "What do you mean?"

"The eye of the Vesica Pisces circle symbolizes the marriage between the feminine and the masculine. It is where harmony and equality have always existed. The two become one, one with the Great Mother Goddess. When that happens, then we will all experience this cataclysmic event throughout our universe. Earth will be the biggest recipient of this newly opened energy channel. The entire planet and all who live on her will be bathed in this glorious, healing energy."

She heard the undisguised excitement in his voice and saw the gleam in his green eyes. "What will that do to the people?"

Shrugging, Nicholas said, "I don't know. This has never happened before, but I'm sure it will be good. We are all witnesses to a great event taking place in Creation."

Mary knew little of the Vesica Pisces but had tried to learn more before the dusk ceremony. Nicholas had explained that the Earth was in a spiral-armed galaxy. It took the Earth's solar system twenty-six thousand years to make one complete circle around the center of the galaxy. There were thirteen thousand years of *Tupay* and heavy energy and the same amount for the *Taqe* energy. They were on the cusp of the change from *Tupay* to *Taqe* energy. It would take place on December 21, 2012. It was hoped that the Emerald Key Necklace would, in some positive way, help the Earth and all its inhabitants who yearned for the light energy instead of hanging on tightly to the heavy *Tupay* energy that now ruled the planet. For everyone, it would become a choice between *Tupay* wars and *Taqe* peace.

The dusk deepened to fuchsia above them. The jungle seemed to quiet. She felt as if all of Creation was now holding its collective breath as Alaria, Ana and Adaire stepped into the eye.

Mary wasn't prepared for what happened next. As they stood facing the east, where the dark cover of night moved toward them, the entire eye lit up with thousands of glittering shafts of light. The white energy surrounded them in the shape of the oval fish eye. Voices from the choir rose; the music deepened. She placed her hand to shield her eyes from the glowing brightness.

Alaria stood on the left side of Ana. Adaire came and faced both of them, the necklace flashing intense green-gold shafts into the white light burning around the edge of the oval. Mary watched as Alaria invoked a prayer of peace and goodwill among all beings on Earth to the Great Mother Goddess. As she lifted her hands in supplication and asked that Ana be allowed not only to wear the necklace, but to become the beacon for all, the sky turned a vivid magenta.

Once Alaria's arms fell to her sides, she turned and picked up the necklace in her aged hands. She lifted it once more to the east and asked for a blessing. Mary thought it was an eloquent symbol that the green and gold flashing from the necklace was sending thousands of shafts of continual light into the approaching darkness. Light instead of darkness. It all made sense to her now.

As Alaria placed the necklace around Ana's neck, Adaire lifted her thick, black hair so that the linked jewels lay against her skin. The necklace settled into place, and Adaire allowed Ana's hair to fall in shining waves against her back. Adaire then moved to Ana's right side. The elders clasped Ana's hands and an explosion of light, color and heavy, throbbing vibrations began.

Mary gasped and gripped Nicholas. His arm automatically tightened around her shoulders.

No longer could Mary see any of the people in the eye. The white light burned bright, and flashes of emerald and gold shot out in thousands of directions. It reminded Mary of a flashing dance ball with hundreds of mirror facets, the light striking each one so that shafts of brightness shot in every direction. The earth beneath them began to tremble and shiver. The voices of the choir continued, strong and beautiful. The music wafted around them.

Mary was riveted, and so was everyone else. It felt to her as if she were in a power substation and electric energy was being sent into it for the first time. Her entire body began to vibrate. The earth beneath her feet shivered continually, but she was not thrown off balance. The sky remained a dark pink, the symbolic color for love and compassion. Mary felt lighter and the instruments and voices all combined to make her feel as if she were in a church. Indeed, they were. But it was the church of the cosmos.

Mary cried with surprise as a beam of light shot down from above. It resembled a flashlight in some ways but she could see people from above walking down in that tunnel of light into the eye of the Vesica Pisces oval. They wore colorful gowns that flowed around their ankles. Ten people came down through this tunnel of light and into the eye.

Stunned, Mary looked up at Nicholas. He shrugged, letting her know he didn't know who they were, either. And then, a very old woman, her long gray hair almost down to her hips, ascended into the beam of light once more. In her hands, she carried the Emerald Key Necklace. As she disappeared into the fuchsia-colored clouds above them, the beam of light suddenly disappeared.

The singing stopped, and the musical instruments fell silent. The blinding white light around the eye ceased. Blinking, Mary saw that Alaria, Adaire and Ana, along with nine other people, remained standing in the eye. Dusk fell upon them. One by one, the people in the eye walked out and moved beyond the Vesica Pisces symbol.

With a wave of his hand, Adaire made a gesture that said "follow me." No one walked into the symbol; that was forbidden. To do so would vibrationally disturb the new energy now pulsing around the individual circles. As Mary walked with Nicholas, her grandfather behind her, red light pulsed around the red rocks, and white energy throbbed around the white. Where they overlapped, all the colors of the rainbow suddenly flashed. It sent beams up into the sky and down into the earth. She was amazed by the beauty as well as the lightness thrumming through every cell in her body.

Everyone gathered in the village center afterward. Darkness had arrived and people had put flaming torches in metal holders so that the main area was lit. Mary noted the look on Ana's face. She glowed, as if not quite real. The smile on her face made Mary want to cry for joy. There was such love emanating from around her that it seemed to move in soft, gentle waves from her heart to everyone in the village.

The nine alien strangers stood smiling, their hands clasped in front of them. They were of different ages and genders. Some appeared to be in their thirties and some much older. There were five men and four women. The fifth woman, the most ancient, had carried the Emerald Key Necklace back to wherever she'd come from. Curiosity was burning in Mary. Who were these people?

Ana sat down on a stool. Her husband, Mace Ridfort, came forward and offered her a glass of juice. Ana smiled, accepted the mug and drank deeply. Mace smiled, too, and sat down next to her. He gripped her hand.

Alaria and Adaire moved toward the people of the village. Alaria raised her voice. "My sisters and brothers, I want you to welcome our kin from the Pleiades." She gestured toward the nine people. "For so long, we have yearned to create contact once more with our home. *Taqe* people originally came from the Pleiades. Those courageous volunteers came here to help Earth turn from *Tupay* heavy energy toward the light energy instead. We owe them more than we can ever repay them." Alaria beamed over at Ana. "At dusk, we were able to complete the first of several mystical steps to bring Earth and all her inhabitants back into the fold of light energy. We owe Ana Ridfort everything. She was not only able to wear the necklace, but to open up the energy channel to allow this Pleiadian assembly to be with us on this momentous occasion."

Ana nodded and humbly acknowledged her husband, Mace. "Thank you, Grandmother. If not for the love of my husband, I would not be able to do this." She touched her swollen belly. "And we pray that our baby will be a compassionate leader to help guide Earth's people back into the light."

"That will happen," Adaire intoned gravely. "The baby you carry now has the seeds of energy not only from Earth, but from the stars. She will be the first of her kind: a new race that will volunteer to be incarnated upon Earth, to intermarry with souls in order to lift the vibration of the planet. And as it lifts, then the Pleiadians can once more help those of Earth in new ways."

Mary marveled at the pronouncement. Mace gave his glowing wife a tender, loving look. They held hands and Mary sighed. The love between them was beautiful. Turning, she gazed up at Nicholas. His eyes met hers, and he shared a tender smile with her. Mary felt his love infuse her. Her arm was around his waist and she gave him a squeeze to let him know she loved him.

"In the coming weeks, as we speak with the Pleiadians," Alaria told them, "we will create a new template for Earth with their help. One that will serve Earth and all its struggling people. We will create a new strategy from our hearts and you will be told of this plan. Be at peace, everyone. Blessings from the Great Mother Goddess upon all of us." Alaria held up her hands and blessed the crowd.

"Well, that's it?" Jeff asked, walking up to them. "The ceremony is over?"

Nicholas nodded. "Yes, it is complete. You must feel good about your part in it."

Jeff smiled a little. "I do, but I don't think I realized the importance of it all."

Mary touched her grandfather's shoulder. "I didn't, either. I know the other people who had missions to find the sphere were here as well. They must feel high from all of this."

Nicholas said, "Come, it's time to eat. Jeff? Will you come to our hut in the morning and break the fast with us?"

"I'd like that. Thank you." Jeff placed a peck on Mary's cheek. "I'll see you tomorrow morning. I love you."

Those softly spoken words melted Mary's heart. She threw her arms around Jeff and gave him a long hug. "I love you, too, Grandfather." Stepping back, she saw his face alight with love for her. Mary also saw relief that his actions had helped bring a new peaceful energy to Earth. "I'm proud of you," she whispered, waving goodbye to him.

As they walked arm in arm back toward their hut, Mary watched as the group of people melted away and went back to their respective abodes. Everyone had been a part of an incredible change in Earth's history. Thirteen thousand years of hatred, prejudice, suppression of women—it would finally start changing for the better. She knew it. She could feel it in her wide-open heart. Nicholas lifted away the dark brown cloth that served as a doorway to their thatched hut.

Inside, a small candle in a clay bowl burned on the wooden table. It shed just enough light so they could see. Mary turned as Nicholas entered. He always had looked so hard and tense, but now his handsome face was relaxed. Love burned in his green, shadowed eyes. Stepping toward him, she slid her arms around his neck. Standing on tiptoe, she whispered against his lips, "I love you…forever."

* * * * *

nocturne™

COMING NEXT MONTH

Available June 29, 2010

#91 ZOMBIE MOON
Lori Devoti

#92 THE VAMPIRE'S KISS
Vivi Anna

HARLEQUIN®

A Romance

FOR EVERY MOOD™

Spotlight on

─ Heart & Home ─

Heartwarming romances
where love can happen
right when you least expect it.

See the next page to enjoy a sneak peek
from Silhouette Special Edition®,
a Heart and Home series.

Introducing McFARLANE'S PERFECT BRIDE
by USA TODAY *bestselling author Christine Rimmer,*
from Silhouette Special Edition®.

Entranced. Captivated. Enchanted.

Connor sat across the table from Tori Jones and couldn't help thinking that those words exactly described what effect the small-town schoolteacher had on him. He might as well stop trying to tell himself he wasn't interested. He was powerfully drawn to her.

Clearly, he should have dated more when he was younger.

There had been a couple of other women since Jennifer had walked out on him. But he had never been entranced. Or captivated. Or enchanted.

Until now.

He wanted her—*her,* Tori Jones, in particular. Not just someone suitably attractive and well-bred, as Jennifer had been. Not just someone sophisticated, sexually exciting and discreet, which pretty much described the two women he'd dated after his marriage crashed and burned.

It came to him that he…he *liked* this woman. And that was new to him. He liked her quick wit, her wisdom and her big heart. He liked the passion in her voice when she talked about things she believed in.

He liked *her.* And suddenly it mattered all out of proportion that she might like him, too.

Was he losing it? He couldn't help but wonder. Was he cracking under the strain—of the soured economy, the McFarlane House setbacks, his divorce, the scary changes in his son? Of the changes he'd decided he needed to make in his life and himself?

Strangely, right then, on his first date with Tori Jones, he didn't care if he just might be going over the edge. He was having a great time—having *fun*, of all things—and he didn't want it to end.

Is Connor finally able to admit his feelings to Tori,
and are they reciprocated?
Find out in McFARLANE'S PERFECT BRIDE
by USA TODAY *bestselling author Christine Rimmer.*
Available July 2010,
only from Silhouette Special Edition®.

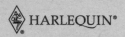
HARLEQUIN®

Showcase

LESLIE KELLY
Naturally Naughty

Wicked & Willing

On sale June 8

Reader favorites from the most talented voices in romance

Save $1.00 on the purchase of 1 or more Harlequin® Showcase books.

SAVE $1.00 on the purchase of 1 or more Harlequin® Showcase books.

Coupon expires November 30, 2010. Redeemable at participating retail outlets.
Limit one coupon per customer. Valid in the U.S.A. and Canada only.

Canadian Retailers: Harlequin Enterprises Limited will pay the face value of this coupon plus 10.25¢ if submitted by customer for this product only. Any other use constitutes fraud. Coupon is nonassignable. Void if taxed, prohibited or restricted by law. Consumer must pay any government taxes. Void if copied. Nielsen Clearing House ("NCH") customers submit coupons and proof of sales to Harlequin Enterprises Limited, P.O. Box 3000, Saint John, NB E2L 4L3, Canada. Non-NCH retailer—for reimbursement submit coupons and proof of sales directly to Harlequin Enterprises Limited, Retail Marketing Department, 225 Duncan Mill Rd., Don Mills, ON M3B 3K9, Canada.

U.S. Retailers: Harlequin Enterprises Limited will pay the face value of this coupon plus 8¢ if submitted by customer for this product only. Any other use constitutes fraud. Coupon is nonassignable. Void if taxed, prohibited or restricted by law. Consumer must pay any government taxes. Void if copied. For reimbursement submit coupons and proof of sales directly to Harlequin Enterprises Limited, P.O. Box 880478, El Paso, TX 88588-0478, U.S.A. Cash value 1/100 cents.

52609057

5 65373 00076 2   (8100)0 11654

® and TM are trademarks owned and used by the trademark owner and/or its licensee.
© 2010 Harlequin Enterprises Limited

HSCCOUP0610